HURLING STICK
TO
FOUNTAIN PENS

War in Ireland 1919-1921

by

Patrick Joseph Sexton

DORRANCE
PUBLISHING CO
EST. 1920
PITTSBURGH, PENNSYLVANIA 15238

Dorrance Publishing Co
585 Alpha Drive
Suite 103
Pittsburgh, PA 15238
Visit our website at www.dorrancebookstore.com

ISBN: 978-1-4809-3507-5
eISBN: 978-1-4809-3530-3

CHAPTER 1

THE PATROL

On a Friday night in 1919 a knock comes on the door of O'-Sullivan's house: A young dispatch carrier hands a message to Mrs. Sullivan for her two sons James and John. It is from Brigadier Lyons. She hands it to James and he begins to read it. It said, "Be at O'Connor's field tomorrow night at 8 P.M. sharp and come armed." They look at each other wondering what this means. They wonder if this could be the action they had longed hoped for. They had joined the Irish Volunteers years before and had drilled and trained for years with the local company of the volunteers, now called the I.R.A. or Irish Republican Army.

They made sure to get a good night's sleep and skipped their usual card games at a neighbour's house. After the family rosary they were in bed by 10 P.M.. The next day, they took it easy around their parents' farm, doing over some light chores. They recovered their rifles from a hiding place they had constructed in

it a hole in the floor and inserted the
Republican literature just under the
er found the hiding place. They didn't
ie guns as she would worry too much
und searching for weapons.

l and oiled their rifles. Very few men
ie Sullivans had managed to scrape to-
gether the price of ~~ ~ ~ rifle. This was like a few months' wages
at the time in most jobs, but they had made the sacrifice and
would be ready for action when needed. They also had managed
to buy some ammunition from time to time and had collected
around one hundred bullets.

They said goodbye to their parents at 7 P.M.. Their mother
sprinkled them with holy water, hugged them both, and wished
them well. Their father shook their hands and said how proud
their Fenian grandfather would have been to see this day. It was
he who passed on to them the Republican tradition of armed resistance to British rule in Ireland. "Good luck, sons," their father
said. "I know you will win."

They knew O'Connor's field really well. They had often
drilled there with the local company and sometimes played football there. They made their way across fields and quiet back roads
to the assembly point. The Brigadier had warned them often
about spies and informers.

Security and secrecy, he used to drill the words into their
brains. Informers had destroyed the Fenians. The I.R.A. would
have to be vigilant, no loose talk, preferably no alcohol. Most of
the men didn't drink alcoholic liquor and indeed a lot of them
were in their late teens. The Sullivans knew every field, every

ditch, and every by-road around their locality, and they soon got to O'Connor's field without being noticed by anybody.

Several men had already assembled, over twenty-two altogether. The Brigadier arrived at 8 P.M. sharp with his friend John O'Dwyer, the company commander. The men gathered around him in a circle and he began to talk.

"Thank you all for coming here tonight. The time for action is here. All the scoffers and cynics who said we would never do anything will have to eat their words. They said we were rainbow chasers, without a stim of sense. What could we do against the mighty British Empire that has just won a great war, with our hurling sticks and silly parades on Sundays? We could never fight. They were wrong. We will fight, but firstly we have to get the weapons needed. We have not enough money to buy them and headquarters in Dublin will only send an occasional revolver or few rounds of ammunition. We have to take them by force from the British. Our intelligence officer has noted a British patrol of ten soldiers regularly entered our parish on foot, armed with rifles and ammunition. We plan to attack them and take the arms from them. We have chosen a stretch of road north of the town where they always travel and we can be sure to ambush them there. We have to assume their rifles are loaded and be careful they don't get to use them. Now ye know why ye practiced jumping over the wall all last week and taking the hurling sticks from your comrades who played the part of the British Patrol.

"We don't want any casualties on either side, because headquarters doesn't want a war started just yet. They hope to get the Republic recognized at the Versailles Conference and no war will be needed. But I know better. This is a vain hope. However, if any man feels his life is in danger he can shoot to save himself. Dublin will have to accept it."

The men made their way in groups of four to the action site. At least one man in each group knew exactly where to go and they all reached the site about 9:30 P.M.

It was a moonlight night, good enough to enable the action to take place. The Brigadier deployed his men along a stretch of road for a hundred yards in pairs. A few men had revolvers and he scattered them along the line to cover hopefully every soldier. He, himself, and John Dwyer took up a position inside a gate they left partially opened. John was a veteran of World War I and a cool, efficient soldier. He was a first class marksman and was a great inspiration for the younger men. He was armed with a parabellum as was the Brigadier. A lot of these weapons had been smuggled into Ireland and were already very popular with the I.R.A. They could be used as miniature rifles when the wooden stock was attached and just like a revolver with the stock removed.

It was very important to capture the leader of the patrol and make sure he didn't escape and make the action's outcome much less certain. For that reason the Brigadier placed a rifleman fifty yards in front to protect against surprise from that direction. Similarly, a rifleman was placed one hundred yards to the rear of the position along the approach road as a precaution against surprise from that direction. The last two men behind the wall were the Sullivan brothers. They had the important task of subduing the last soldiers and making sure they didn't retreat back along the road. The Brigadier was confident that he had covered all eventualities so nothing was left now except wait for the patrol.

This was always the hardest part, not knowing if they would come or not. All sorts of things crowded the men's thoughts going back to their younger days. They were ordered to maintain silence, no smoking was allowed, and to stay very low crouched behind the wall. Each man knew they would be in harm's way and this could be their last night in this world.

It was almost 11 P.M. and suddenly the word was passed along the line that the patrol had arrived: ten men as expected. Each man pressed hard against the wall, ready to scale it at the signal, a whistle from the Brigadier.

The patrol was led by a burly sergeant. They were completely off guard. Nobody had attacked them for months and they didn't expect any difference tonight. When the sergeant was almost at the gate, the Brigadier and John Dwyer sprung out of the gate and knocked the sergeant down. At the same time, Lyons blew the whistle. All the I.R.A. men jumped the wall and attacked the nearest soldier. Dwyer held the sergeant in a chokehold and Lyons pointed his gun at him. "Surrender or shoot, and order your men to surrender". He realized he was beaten and said yes. He surrendered and ordered the men to do the same.

Some soldiers tried to resist, but they were overpowered in five minutes. The last soldier tried to escape, but the Sullivans were onto him right away. John tripped him and James used the butt of his rifle on the man's head. This stunned him long enough for the Sullivans to grab his gun. The soldiers were lined against the roadside wall, stripped of their rifles, and ammunition, and forced to go into a nearby farmer's shed.

They were locked in there and would only get out when the farmer came to milk his cows around 6 A.M. next day. They were warned not to punish the farmer as he was not involved in the plans and didn't actually live on the farm but in another farm a mile away.

Meanwhile the I.R.A. made their getaway with the rifles and ammunition. They gave them to their quartermaster, who had prepared a special dump for the weapons. Each man was told to go home right away as the police would be out raiding for the participants next morning.

The Brigadier left to go to a safe house four miles away, and all the others went home, hoping to bluff their way.

The Sullivans arrived home at 2:30 A.M.. Their mother was overjoyed to see them. She made tea for them and urged them to go to bed as next day was Sunday and they would be up for Mass at 11A.M.. Only one I.R.A. man was wounded. He was brought to a doctor who treated him and he stayed in a safe house for a week until he recovered. He had a cover story for the police, if they called. His parents would say he went to Dublin for a wedding and week's holiday.

Sure enough, the police were busy next morning with their enquiries. They checked their list of the usual suspects and the Sullivans were high on the top of it. They knocked on the Sullivans' door at 9 A.M.. Their mother opened the door.

"Where are your sons?" the R.I.C. sergeant said.

"Right here in the kitchen eating breakfast," she replied.

"Where were ye last night?" asked the R.I.C. man. "Don't tell us ye were playing cards at the neighbours, as we checked that already."

"We were at home all night. We had a hard week at work and worked very hard at the turf yesterday so we turned in early," replied James.

Mrs. Sullivan confirmed the story.

"We will check you both for wounds or scratches. If we find any ye are going to jail," said the sergeant. They went into a bedroom and the police examined them in detail and found nothing. They had hidden the clothes they used the night before and washed themselves and put on their best suits.

"Alright," said the sergeant. "We have found nothing that will hold up in court so ye are free this time. If there are any more incidents like the patrol attack ye are going away for a long stretch."

The British government pretended the problem in Ireland was just a law and order problem that the police should handle. But it was getting out of hand. Too many police had resigned already and new recruits were harder to get. They would have to bring over men from England, Scotland and Wales to shore up the R.I.C. They still would not admit a state of war existed. Meanwhile the I.R.A. continued to organize and get stronger and stronger. The majority of the people backed them and there was a real hope of success this time.

CHAPTER 2

THE R.I.C.

The R.I.C. completed their inquiries in about two weeks. They had their suspects but no evidence. They could not lock up all the young men in the parish. It was getting harder to get information. Informers could expect no mercy especially if the information led to the death of an I.R.A. man. Nobody went to prison for the patrol attack. The local people were elated over the success. Every company member begged to be part of the next action. The R.I.C. still thought they would suppress the rebellion as they had done in 1867 when they beat the Fenians. A grateful Queen of England, Victoria, called them the Royal Irish Constabulary in gratitude. They lived in barracks all over Ireland. Nearly every town or village had its barracks. They kept a close watch on all the Irish Organizations like Sinn Fein, I.R.A., Gaelic League, GAA, and Cumann Na Mban and regularly sent reports to Dublin Castle.

About two weeks after the patrol attack Brigadier Lyons arrived in the locality again. He summoned a meeting attended by

John Dwyer, the two Sullivans, and Dowd, the company intelligence officer. He had formed a high opinion of all those men and expected them to play important parts in all his future plans.

The meeting was held upstairs in a private room above a pub in the town. The Publican, a man of about fifty was a staunch supporter and had contributed generously to the Sinn Fein candidate for the Dail in the 1918 election. His place was always open to the I.R.A. for meetings.

"Boys," the Brigadier said to his men. "We have had enough of the R.I.C. harassment. They are the main enemies of Irish freedom at this point and we have to fight them."

"They will not give in without a fight," Dowd said. "Are they not Irish like ourselves? And Irishmen are by nature fighters!"

"That might be true," said Lyons. "And we have to stop them or they will destroy us."

"How many R.I.C. men are in the local barracks?" asked the Brigadier.

"About 15" said the intelligence officer.

"No doubt they all have a rifle each and loads of ammunition. It would be great if we could capture the place," said the Brigadier. "Describe its defenses."

The British had begun to fortify all the barracks in the brigade area. They evacuated a lot of the smaller barracks, before the I.R.A. could grab their weapons. This barrack was a two-story stone structure. The doors had been reinforced with steel and the windows with steel shutters.

Several loopholes were cut in both the front and back, to enable the police to fire at any attackers. The gables had no loopholes as yet, but sometimes they cut holes and put a light cover of plaster over them that could be easily broken out in a fight. They had sandbags in every room to use to put out any fires.

The I.R.A. was very short of explosives to blow a hole in the wall, so the only hope was to go up on the roof, break holes in the slates, and set fire to the upper floors, using lighted sods of turf soaked in paraffin or petrol. Sledge-hammers would be used and lump-hammers to break holes in the slates and buckets of paraffin used to splash the liquid into the upper rooms.

"How can we get on the roof?" asked James Sullivan. "The roof is forty feet high on the open end of the structure."

"We will tie some ladders together and climb up. The other gable-end is connected to a general store. We can break into that, go via the skylight, and crawl onto the roof of the barracks and attack it like that. All our supplies can be brought up in the store," said Lyons.

"So we will light sods of turf and use them as blazing torches to burn the barracks." Said Dowd. "I never imagined sods of turf would be used as weapons, but it seems reasonable. I say let's do it."

The next day word was sent to thirty men to gather at a disused farmhouse and begin training to attack the barracks. One volunteer had been in the British Navy and he was very good at making knots, so he tied the ladders together to reach up forty feet. Four ladders would be used to get onto the roof on the detached gable of the barracks, making two long ladders. The Sullivan brothers were chosen to climb these ladders that would rest against the ledge either side of the chimney. A crew of men practiced carrying the ladders and standing them against the side of a haybarn which would be roughly the height of the barracks. When the Brigadier was happy that this part of the attack was fully understood and mastered, he set a date for the attack.

Tins of petrol and paraffin were collected, as were bags of turf and several empty buckets. There was paraffin in the general store which they planned to commandeer and use on the roof. Brigadier Lyons and John Dwyer would climb onto the roof through the general store and break as many holes as possible. Hopefully they would make enough holes on their side of the roof and the Sullivans enough holes on the other side to get a really good fire started that the police could not extinguish.

The night of the attack came and was dry and windy. The ladder crew carried the ladders across fields to the barracks gable end. The ex-navy man began to knot them together. The ladder crew lifted the ladder against the gable end. Two men with revolvers covered them, in case of loopholes, and no fire came from the barracks. Now it was the turn of the Sullivans. They were a strange sight, weighed down with a tin of paraffin each, sods of turf carried around their neck with cords, grenades, matches, and a lump-hammer tied to their wrists. They climbed onto the roof and began to break holes in the roof with their lump-hammers. On the other end the Brigadier and O'Dwyer climbed through the skylight and onto the roof and started breaking holes.

The attack was timed to start at twelve midnight and riflemen at the front and back kept up a steady fire to mask the hammering on the roof. They were ordered to keep this up for twenty minutes and by then the men on the roof should have enough holes made to start a good blaze in the upper floor.

The police fired their Verey light pistols in the hope of alerting nearby police posts, but no help came. The phone lines were cut so no call was possible. The Brigadier had men watching the approach roads to stop any relief force. They had cut trenches and in some cases felled trees as obstacles. The British hated to travel at night, so there was plenty of time before daylight to capture the barracks.

James Sullivan moved along the roof to about the half-way mark and soon had a hole made. John broke a hole closer to the chimney. He was lucky as the room under him was occupied by two policemen who dated local girls. They were arrested by the I.R.A. before they could return that night.

The sergeant realized that men were on the roof trying to break-in. He sent two men upstairs to fire at them. They missed. James tossed in a grenade and John Dwyer fired through a hole he had made on his side. They lit their sods of turf and tossed them in the holes. There was a big explosion and smoke billowed through the holes. The police gave up firing and retreated downstairs. There was too much smoke to endure staying upstairs. The Brigadier gave the order to get down. The barrack could not be saved now.

The Sullivans climbed down. Some of their hair was burned off. Their faces were blackened, their hands blistered, and their eyebrows singed.

"My God," said the Brigadier. "Ye must be fireproof the way the wind blew the flames around ye." The Brigadier and Dwyer also had burns, but they forgot their pain as they sensed victory.

The Brigadier called on the police to surrender. "We will spare your lives if you come out now. Throw out the guns and boxes of ammunition." The sergeant agreed and they threw out the guns and ammunition and some of the grenades and revolvers with .45 and .32 ammunition.

They marched out with their hands up and were made to cross the street and stand with their hands against the wall of a house. The I.R.A. men checked to make sure they had no hidden weapons.

Ten men rushed into the barracks and found a few more boxes of ammunition and a box of grenades. They just got out before the ceiling of the upper floor fell down. The slated roof followed soon after.

"I'm afraid ye will have to look for new lodgings," said the Brigadier to Sergeant Roche, the leader of the R.I.C. He wrote down their names and warned them if they were captured again they would not get off so lightly. Many of the volunteers wanted to shoot them, but Lyons had given his word. However he could not resist having a little fun with them as he recalled being harassed by them and once sent to prison because of their evidence. He decided a bit of drill would be great. "Fall in," he roared. "Forward march, left right, left right, halt, about turn, halt, stand at ease." This was on for fifteen minutes. The sergeant was reluctant, but a revolver pressed against his temple changed his mind. The townspeople peered through their windows, astonished by the change in times and humiliation of the R.I.C. The R.I.C. were locked in the National School.

"Ye will be released by the principal next morning at 9 A.M.," Lyons said.

The volunteers removed the weapons and hurried them to dumps miles away. The Brigadier thanked the men for their success. The outposts went home at daybreak. Most of the I.R.A. went to their homes. Lyons, Dwyer, and the two Sullivans made their way to the far end of the brigade. From then on the Sullivans and Dwyer would be on the run like Lyons. They could no longer live at home. The police were released next morning and were picked up by a British patrol and brought to a bigger barrack in a nearby town.

The barrack could no longer be used. No local workers would help to renovate it if they valued their lives. A large area around the town was now free from the prying eyes of the R.I.C.

They might be in a barrack ten miles away, but now they would have to travel a greater distance to make a raid and capture someone. Travel was dangerous for the British. There could be an ambush at any turn of the road. Obstructions were numerous, such as trenches and blown bridges. Now the area would be a great area for rest and recuperation for the volunteers. The British would have to do something soon to boost the police and they had a plan: send in the Black-and-Tans.

CHAPTER 3

THE BLACK AND TANS

The English government set up offices to recruit men for the R.I.C. in Glasgow and Liverpool. There were loads of unemployed men in England at the time, mostly ex-servicemen from the World War. They returned home to a "land fit for heroes," but found they could get no work. There was a chance to go somewhere and do something and police work in Ireland would look attractive. The pay was very good: ten shillings a day all found. They began to arrive in Ireland in March of 1920 and by September two thousand had arrived, bringing the R.I.C. up to ten thousand men by September of 1920.

They could not find enough of the R.I.C. uniforms so they wore a mixture of either black tunics and khaki trousers or black trousers and khaki tunics. Somebody called them the Black-and-Tans after a pack of hounds in Limerick and the name stuck. They were ordered to make Ireland a "hell for rebels to live in" and took their job very seriously. Before they were finished in 1921 they had made Ireland a hell for everyone to live in, even unionists.

The R.I.C. was no longer concerned with ordinary police work like catching cattle rustlers, land grabbers, and all kinds of petty criminals. They didn't care anymore. The I.R.A. and its court system took care of that. Now the R.I.C. concentrated on chasing the I.R.A.

The Tans and R.I.C. would live together in strongly fortified barracks and from there travel around the local area searching for I.R.A. men. There was a criminal element amongst the Tans, and if they didn't feel like paying for drinks or groceries, or anything else for that matter, they just robbed Ireland at gunpoint.

There was no discipline enforced by the British government. If they killed any Irish person or destroyed their houses, no questions were asked.

The Sullivan brothers had been on the run for months. They decided to go home to see their parents. The Brigadier didn't like the idea but liked them so much he said they could do it.

"Don't stay overnight. All it takes is one informer and ye will be in trouble. Ye know what the British will do if they catch ye. Ye are high on the wanted list."

They made their way to their local town and passed the ruin of the barracks they had captured. The day was warm and sunny and they got very thirsty. They decided to have a drink in Clancy's pub, where they had often met other I.R.A. men and held the meeting to decide the attack on the barracks. Clancy was behind the counter and was stunned to see the two of them. He greeted them warmly and put two drinks before them on the counter.

"What are ye doing in this town, boys?" he asked.

"We are here to visit our parents. Our parents have not seen us for months and our mother has been sick lately. We hope for a quick visit and then we will move on again," they said.

"I will send a messenger to them to expect ye tonight," Clancy replied.

Just then a young man came in to the pub and ordered a pint of Guinness. They knew him from National School, but they had not seen him for years. His name was John Garry. They recognized each other and shook hands.

James asked him, "Where have you been?"

"I was in the British Army and fought in the Middle East and France. I got wounded in 1918 and spent some time in hospital. When I recovered the war was over and I was demobilised in 1919 and came back to Ireland."

"What are you doing now?" John asked.

"I'm studying accounting in the hope of getting a good job. I should qualify in a few months. So what are you boys doing?"

"We are working at carpentry, but things are a bit slack right now. We are between jobs," James replied.

They were careful not to mention the I.R.A. He might have been hostile or he might have been sympathetic. Some veterans were great and joined the I.R.A., and some were outright hostile and worked for the British or just did nothing at all.

"Have you been following the political situation?" Clancy asked.

"Yes," he said. "The rebellion was a great shock for me. I knew no Irish history. I had never heard of Pearse, Connolly, Clarke, or any of the leaders. What did they want rising like that? I lived up to my commitment to the army until demobilised. Then I studied Irish history in earnest."

"Have you reached a conclusion?" James asked.

"Yes," he said. "I am in favour of the fight for Irish freedom. It is the way to go. TheBritish will not just walk away from Ireland."

"Do you like the idea enough maybe to help the movement?" John asked.

"You mean to join the I.R.A.?" said Garry."Yes, I would be prepared to join if I knew who to talk to."

Clancy said, "That deserves a drink on the house." And he put three more drinks before them."

James said, "We are members ourselves. We have to talk to our Brigadier before we do anymore. We will send you an answer in a few days." The boys knew a man like Garry would make a great training officer which the Brigade badly needed for they knew they had to proceed with caution.

Just then they heard a screeching noise outside the pub. Clancy glanced through the window and saw a Tan lorry outside. It was too late to run out the back, as the Tans were already on the way in the front door.

"Keep cool boys" he said. "Bluff your way."

"Gentlemen," he said to the Tans. "What can I do for ye?"

They ordered drinks and Clancy said, "This is on the house." He wanted to start off on a good note. He had no idea what they knew. There was no R.I.C. man with them thankfully. The drinks put them in a good humour. The leader asked Clancy who the three men were.

"I don't know who they are," replied the barman. "I never saw them before today. They could be commercial travelers maybe."

John Garry pulled some identification out of his pocket and showed it to the Tan leader.

"So I see you were in the British army and fought in France and Iraq," said the leader. John rolled up his right sleeve and showed the effects of bullet wounds he received. One of the Tan group had been in France and asked a few questions about place names and regiments. John had been there and his answers satisfied the Tans that he was proving still loyal to England.

"There are my friends from national school," He said, pointing to the Sullivans. "They are carpenters working for a building firm." There was an all round sigh of relief as the answers seemed to satisfy the Tans.

They had just come to the Brigade area but had seen no action yet. Nobody had fired a shot at them. They had come across a trench on the main road into the town but forced some locals to fill it in. Apart from that this was a nice assignment and in comparison with World War I it was a breeze.

"What do ye think of the political situation in the country?" asked the leader. Clancy spoke up at this point.

"I'm sorry," he said. "But I discourage political talk in my pub. We had some trouble here before the 1918 election between Home Rulers and Sinn Feiners, not to mention the unionists. It led to some fights and I banned some trouble makers. The conversation can be about horse-racing, football, hurling, soccer, cattle prices, but no politics. Anyone who wants to enjoy a drink here has to respect that."

"All right," replied the Tan leader. "We will not discuss politics."

One of his colleagues said, "You can hardly expect any locals to spy on their neighbours as the penalty is death if caught by the

I.R.A." Some informers had been executed already in other parts of the Brigade. It was now 5 P.M. and the Tan leader said, "We had better make our way back to our barracks for supper."

They finished their drinks and left the pub. Garry and the Sullivans also finished their drinks and left the bar.

Garry headed for his parents' home about a mile away, and a pony and trap picked up the Sullivans and took them to see their parents. The driver dropped them at the house and said, "I will be back in two hours to collect ye." Their parents were so delighted to see them. Their mother kissed and hugged them and their father shook their hands. He congratulated them for their part in taking the local barracks. Local I.R.A. volunteers had given him the whole story.

Their mother had a big meal ready for them: bacon, cabbage, potatoes, tea, and bread and butter.

They were ravenous and sat down at the kitchen table to eat their fill.

"Mama, we heard you were sick," James said.

"I had the flu," she replied. "But I have recovered thanks to our local doctor."

"I pray for ye night and day, that ye will survive this war and come back home safe to us," she said.

"We can't stay long," John said. "Only two hours!" The two hours passed quickly and they had to leave. Their father shook their hands. "Good luck now," he said and their mother sprinkled them with holy water and watched the pony and trap leave until it was out of sight. They spent the night in a safe house on the other side of the parish.

Next day a jaunting car brought them to the parish six miles away where Lyons and O'Dwyer were in billets. They used three scouts on bicycles ahead of them to ensure they would not be caught. If the lead scout saw any trouble up ahead he would signal to the scout behind him and so on back to the jaunting car. Then they could take some evasive action to get by the obstacle. They knew every side road and short cut to use if necessary.

"Welcome back," said Lyons. "How is Mrs. Sullivan?"

"She is fine," they replied. They told him of their adventure with the Tans and how they were not detected.

"Ye were lucky Sergeant Roche was not with the patrol that day," said Lyons. They learned later he had been with another patrol to another town.

"We met an interesting character called John Garry in the pub. We knew him in national school. He is from our parish but has been away in France and the Middle East with the British army. He has lots of military experience. We sounded him out and he seems to be for the Republic now. He is interested in joining us. What do ye think?"

Neither Lyons nor O'Dwyer could remember him as he was a few years younger than them.

"Alright," said Lyons. "We will look him over. Send him a message to meet us here at this house in two nights, Friday at 8 P.M.. They sent the message and he showed up as promised.

Chapter 4

John Garry Signs On

John Garry knocked on the door of the billet at 8 P.M. sharp. The Sullivans greeted him and introduced him to Lyons and O'Dwyer. After some small talk they got around to business in the parlour. The parlour was the cleanest room in the house, reserved for special occasions, like if a yank home from America visited. There was a long talk and they took their seats with the Brigadier at the head.

"The Sullivans tell me you want to join us and fight for Ireland. Why did you join the British Army and what made you change your mind and leave it?" Lyons asked. He was very cautious about newcomers. The British had tried to infiltrate spies into a battallion in a nearby brigade and they almost bagged the leadership there.

"I was shocked by 1916 and in particular the executions. I concluded I was in the wrong army but now I hope to make up for it. I studied Irish history when I got back and learned of Ireland's suffering for seven hundred years. It is time to turn the tables on the British. A majority of the people want independence now. Home rule is no longer good enough," he said.

The Brigadier was pleased with what he heard. He explained how the brigade needed a good training officer with military experience to train a lot of men quickly. They planned to set up a series of training courses, each lasting a week, at different locations around the brigade area.

Each of the seven battalions in the brigade would send at least four officers for training to each camp and when the course was complete each camp would try to engage the British in an ambush or in an attack or a barrack.

The new attacking unit would be called an active service unit, later to become better known as a Flying Column. The column would stay active full-time so at all times a number of I.R.A. men would be ready to attack. There would be no respite for the British now. Prior to now men on the run moved around the county in small groups, often as individuals. As war developed more and more men had to go on the run. It was better to have them move together, find billets together in close proximity, and fight together when an opportunity presented itself.

Each company would have to assist the flying column, when it arrived in its area. Each battalion had three or four companies, depending on the population of the battalion area. They would find food and billets, post sentries, employ scouts, and generally help in any way the column asked for. The column commander would be the boss and had to be obeyed without question. No matter who served in the column, regardless of rank in a battalion, he would have to take orders from the column commander.

A company captain might find himself taking orders from one of his rank and file subordinates, who might be a section commander with the column.

"I joined the British army because I was young, non-political,, and was curious to see what war was like" said Garry. "I am ready to take the job of training officer, but I have reservations about becoming column commander. Maybe the men will not accept that."

"Nonsense," said the Brigadier. "They will be glad to have you, with your experience and youthful enthusiasm. An injection of fresh blood is what is needed."

The meeting was concluded and they sent Garry over to the kitchen, where a nice cup of tea awaited him. They debated among themselves what to do.

The Sullivans and John Dwyer were all for swearing him in to the I.R.A. and making him the training officer. Lyons agreed but took it a step further.

"I believe we should offer him the position of column commander," he said. They looked at the Brigadier with a surprise look on their faces.

"That will mean that you, as Brigadier, and I, as Vice-Brigadier, will have to take orders from him when we serve with the column and we will serve with the column at least some of the time" said O'Dwyer.

"We are all comrades in arms here," replied Lyons. "We need a younger man than me as I am pushing thirty. I think he is ideal at twenty-three or so." After that they decided to offer him the job.

They called him in to the parlour. "You are accepted in the I.R.A. as a training officer, but we also want you for the job of column commander. Do you accept?"

Garry was surprised but was very proud of the offer and the trust they placed in him.

"Alright," he said. "I agree to take the job."

"That is great," said Lyons. "No matter who serves with the column he will accept your orders. That goes for all of us here in this room and for every volunteer in the Brigade area. After

this Lyons swore him in with the oath to the republic. He swore to oppose all enemies of the Republic domestic and foreign. Lyons said they would start a training camp in a week after he sent word to each battalion to select officers for it.

CHAPTER 5

TRAINING CAMP

A week later on a Saturday evening at 7 P.M. the camp began. Officers from each battalion in the brigade cycled to the training centre. Many had to travel up to fifty miles to get there for the weather was good and all these were young, fit men. A college used to hold a big meeting every year of Gaelic language scholars. They came from all over the country to brush up on their Irish.

Some volunteers were teachers and also members of the Gaelic League, so it was a good cover to use this gathering of Irish speaking enthusiasts.

Some of the scholars would sleep in the college and more in tents around the school grounds. The I.R.A. volunteers brought ground sheets, blankets, spare shirts, and socks. They could mix with the students if the police or army came snooping around.

There was a merchant named Casey in a nearby town and he owned a house, some outhouses, and fifty acres of land near the college. He was a great friend of the I.R.A. and allowed them to use his house and fields to train. He lived in the town but planned to retire to his house later in life. It was a good idea to bring officers together from over the brigade area so they could get to know each other and build up brigade spirit. The men gathered in the front lawn of Casey's house and waited for the column commander.

Brigadier Lyons stood before the group and said, "I would like to introduce the new column commander. The Brigade staff has interviewed him and decided he is the man for the job, so here he is."

"My name is John Garry and I would like to thank the staff for giving me the honour of becoming training officer and column commander. I plan to set up a series of training camps in the brigade and train about 150 officers from the seven battalions of the Brigade. In that way each of these officers can return to their battalions and train their company commanders, and so on down to section level so that each man in the brigade is ready to be a competent guerilla fighter.

"By staying in existence we will be a menace to the British. They will never be sure when we will attack. It could be around any bend, on any road, in a village street or town street. We will decide when and where to attack, or we will decline battle if a good retreat is required. It will be a tough existence in a flying column. There will be long marches of fourteen or fifteen miles as we cannot stay too long in any one townland. We will eat when we can find food and accept accommodation whenever we can find it.

"We will sleep in haybarns and outhouses and sometimes in the open. There will be a constant risk of being surrounded and annihilated. I have no need to tell ye arms and ammunition are scarce. Our actions will have to be short, unless we can radically improve the ammunition situation.

"Every company will have to help us when we come to their area. They will provide us with scouts, sentries, and trenching help to hamper British movements. They will find good billets for us and the girls of Cumann Na Mban will supply and cook food for us. This is the people's war. Most of them will help us, but we have to look out for informers. Loose talk will be discouraged and drinking frowned upon. I believe we will not get any approval from the bishops for our campaign. Some of them call us murderers and threaten to excommunicate us for participation in an ambush. So if anyone has any religious scruples, let him leave now. I know ye all must be hungry, so I will end my speech. We will begin training in the morning." With that he sat down and the men went for an evening meal.

Training began early on Sunday. A priest came and heard the confessions of any volunteer who wanted it and said mass in the gymnasium of the school. After mass they had breakfast and then the training began. There was close order drill and extended order drill. They had to learn to obey orders right away and move the way he wanted them. He drilled the word "security" into their heads. They had to learn to act quickly when danger came. They used to have sudden alarms, even at night, and they had to be down at defensive positions in five minutes flat. They had to learn how to keep their heads down and he made them crawl along the ground.

He had a bag full of clay balls and fired them at the back of anyone that didn't keep close enough to the ground. "Learn to love the earth," he shouted. "It can save your lives from the bullets and grenade splinters flying above."

James whispered to John Sullivan, "I feel like I am swallowing earth." Garry picked up a rifle after the men had crawled to the end of the field. He took a glass bottle and gave it to James.

"Put it on the pier of the gate over there." The pier was about five feet high. He took careful aim and shot that bottle into bits. Now he said that could be a man, and he would probably be a dead man already. After the long crawl, he let them stop. They gathered in a group in the middle of the field.

The column commander roared at them. "Scatter out into four groups and go to the corner of the field, and post sentries. If the British appeared behind the wall over there we would all be dead now. This could happen if a scout is captured or security fails to warn us." They saw the sense of this and formed four groups.

The Sullivans, Lyons, and John Dwyer were in one corner. They were all exhausted. The Sullivans did security while the detail rested, and after half an hour, Dwyer and Lyons returned the favour. An hour passed and they had to do more drilling and by 6 P.M. a halt was called to the day's activities. After supper they were glad to turn in.

On Monday there was more drilling and learning to move. One group moved and the other covered them. Then there were sprints, push-ups, and frog-jumping. On Tuesday there were instructions on scouting and engineering and they went for a long march, doing several miles around Casey's farm.

Wednesday came and all this activity must have been brought to the notice of the police and army. The scouts and sentries sent word that the college had been surrounded. The column had their rifles in dumps in the area, cared for by the local company. So they decided to bluff their way. They mingled with the scholars in the college so no stranger could know who the I.R.A. members were and who the genuine scholars were. Hours went by as the British questioned everyone. The local R.I.C. recognized three I.R.A. men and arrested them. That seemed to satisfy them and they withdrew. The I.R.A. men were sentenced to four months in jail.

The British still made a pretense of treating the whole problem as a law and order one, requiring evidence, witnesses, etc. On Thursday, every man collected a rifle from the dumps and ammunition. The commander demonstrated the use of a Lee Enfield rifle, loaded it, pointed it, and fired a shot. Any man who had not yet fired a rifle was allowed to fire three shots at different ranges. That covered about half of the group.

"Don't worry too much about accuracy," said Garry. "We will be keeping so close to the British that you can't miss." On the Friday he allowed each officer to drill a small number of his comrades to get experience of being in charge of men. They fought some sham battles. One group posed as British soldiers and the other group counteracted their moves and vice versa. By Friday night Garry was satisfied he had imparted as much knowledge as he could. The men were glad the course was over, proud of the chance to play their parts as officers and were now ready for guerilla war.

Garry addressed them, thanked them for their effort, and said, "Have a good meal and a good night's sleep. Tomorrow we will leave here and march around in the hope of laying an ambush in some suitable spot."

He divided the group into four sections of eight men and appointed four section commanders: Liam Lyons, John O'Dwyer,

James Sullivan, and John Sullivan. John O'Dowd, the Brigade intelligence officer, and John Garrett, the quarter master, were also
in this column. All of them eagerly awaited the chance to advance
the fight for Irish freedom,

CHAPTER 6

AMBUSH AT BALLYROE

It was no easy matter to meet and ambush a British Patrol in spite of the fact they moved around the Brigade area a lot. They moved at unpredictable times and by routes that were hard to predict. However, there were some examples of movement between certain hours or certain days and these were carefully noted by the Brigade intelligence officer through his network. He reported this to Commander Garry and asked him to check out a place called Ballyroe in the fourth battalion area. He travelled there with Liam Lyons and O'Dowd. There was a road running east-west for about two hundred yards. On either side were low hillocks that would provide a view across country. There were roadside ditches to give cover. There was a hill of about five hundred feet some distance north of the road with a good view of the approach road from the west. The nearest barracks was eight miles to the west and another seven miles to the east. They were far away enough, that gunfire would not be heard so no reinforcements would come. A patrol used to travel between these towns on Wednesday and the column commander decided to attack at this spot. The area was not great for a retreat if necessary as it consisted of a lot of bogland without walls of any sort. However, he believed the British would not follow them into bogland if a retreat was necessary. He decided to attack along a stretch of road extending for about two hundred yards.

On Tuesday night he informed the column about the proposed ambush. They all had a good meal and went to bed at 11 P.M.. They were up and ready to march at 5 A.M. the next day. They had to march six miles to the ambush position and were all in positions by 8 A.M.. Each man carried a rifle and fifty rounds of ammunition. A few had revolvers and the column also had five grenades.

Garry had to decide how to deploy his men. There was no way to know how many lorries would show up. Sometimes one lorry came over; on occasion three lorries travelled. He had to deploy his men to take account of this. The first problem to be solved was how to stop the first lorry. He arranged for a trench to be dug on the eastern end of the ambush position. It was dug during the night by the local company and cleverly camouflaged. This would stop the first lorry.

South of the road behind the ditch he placed six men. James Sullivan had two men to the left of the trench and John Sullivan had two to the right. He hoped with the element of surprise to deal quickly with this group of about twelve to fifteen soldiers. If a second lorry appeared he placed the men under his own command about half way between the extreme ends of the positions. At the western end the road turned northwards and at the eastern end to the south. This group would attack the second lorry but would be flexible and ready to move and help the Sullivan group to the right of them or the Lyons group to the left of them.

At the extreme west end of the position he placed ten men, south of the road near the corner. They could fire along the approach road and eastwards if necessary. This group was under Brigadier Lyons.

The flanks had to be covered in case of surprise from the east or west. No lorry was expected from the east, but he placed John O'Dowd at the bend east of the trench and near Sullivan's group. He could fire on any lorry from the east and hold them up until reinforced.

He placed five men, including the Vice-Brigadier John O'Dwyer, on the five hundred foot hill They had a good view of the approach road and could fire on the main ambush position as well.

The distance to the approach road was one hundred yards and about the same to the east-west stretch of the road.

The commander explained to each group what was expected of them and they all settled in to wait for the British. Everyone had to stay in cover and wait for the signal to fire. This attack would start when the first lorry reached the Sullivan group. Then everyone could fire at wherever target presented itself. There was little traffic on the road. Any passerby, if they noticed anything unusual, pretended they did not and hurried on. One of the column men took a mental note of these passersby as he was a local and knew most of them. You could never be sure one of them would not rush to the barracks and report the presence of the column but it was a risk to be taken.

The column commander visited each group and warned them not to show themselves, or fire too soon, as they could destroy the whole ambush plan.

Nine came, and ten, and eleven o'clock. The men wondered would they come at all. At twelve o'clock the scouts signaled the approach of three lorries from the west. The men pressed hard against the ground and the ditches. Now all their training would be put to the test.

The first lorry came along not suspecting anything. They drove into the trench and stopped. The Sullivan group fired volley after volley and John threw a grenade. It exploded and killed the driver and occupants of the cab. Some of the soldiers in the back sitting on benches were killed but a few jumped down and began to fire back. One of them tried to escape north of the road but he was shot by O'Dowd after he had gone about one hundred yards. In about ten minutes the Sullivans called out "surrender" and they agreed and dropped their rifles. They stood against the lorries. The Sullivan group picked up the rifles and ammunition and pulled away the dead and wounded enemy. They prepared the lorry for burning.

Meanwhile the second lorry had come in front of the column commander's position. He shot the driver and another volunteer threw a grenade that exploded among the soldiers sitting in the back of the lorry. Some were killed and the rest fired back as best they could. After half of their members were killed, Garry called on them to surrender and they agreed. Garry's group collected the rifles ammunition and grenades and pulled aside the dead and wounded and prepared the lorry for burning.

The third lorry stopped just north of the western bend. Lyon's group opened fire on them as did John O'Dwyer from the hill and his group, but the soldiers put up a stubborn resistance. They managed to inflict some wounds on Lyon's group. Garry realized they needed help. He left five men to guard the soldiers of the second lorry, and he called on the Sullivans to join him to attack the third lorry. They left four men to guard the soldiers of the first lorry, and moved along inside the southern wall and with some of Garry's group joined Liam Lyons.

The soldiers noticed the increased fire coming from the Lyons group. John Sullivan took careful aim and shot the lieutenant in charge of the soldiers. His death discouraged the rest.

They saw no help was coming from the other lorries. They decided to surrender and held up a white flag. Garry called on them to throw down their rifles and step away from the lorry. They did so right away. The I.R.A. men collected the rifles and ammunition, pulled away the dead and wounded from the lorry, and prepared it for burning. They prepared the lorries for burning and made the three groups of soldiers come together near the second lorry position.

By now all three lorries were burning. A medic tended to the wounded. The I.R.A. men who were wounded were able to walk to where a doctor gave them medical attention. Garry spoke to the soldiers. This regiment had made a bad name for themselves already. They had murdered some I.R.A. men and burned houses. He warned them if they continued, they would get no mercy next time around. Their sergeant promised to let his superiors know and protested his innocence.

Garry decided to collect his men and get away from there as quickly as possible. The ambush was a great success. The men fought like veterans. They captured almost forty rifles, thousands of rounds of .303 ammunition, a few revolvers, and several boxes of grenades.

Garry addressed his men and praised them for their success. They were all tired, hungry, and thirsty but elated by their success. They began a march across country to billets about ten miles away. They knew they had to put a safe distance between them and the ambush site, as the place would be swarming with troops before the day was over. Several lorries came later that day to collect the dead and wounded. The British would conceal their losses, but they admitted ten dead and six wounded. By 4 P.M. the I.R.A. was ten miles away and enjoying their new billets.

That night, the sergeant who had promised so faithfully to behave, led his men to the nearest town and burned several houses belonging to supporters of the I.R.A.

CHAPTER 7

INFORMERS MUST GO

The Sullivans had heard it often enough around the kitchen fire, from their Fenian grandfather. He used to say "the informers destroyed the Fenian movement." The Brigade had suffered a higher number of casualties than usual in the last month before the ambush. Ten volunteers had been killed by the British army and fifteen taken prisoner, and were awaiting a trial, which would most likely lead to execution. There was no Geneva Convention protection for an I.R.A. man caught in action or with a gun. Some regiments would take prisoners, but the Sussex regiment just murdered men where they found them. It was obvious that a well-organized group of spies were operating. The I.R.A. had to locate and eliminate this group or be wiped out.

A Brigade Council meeting was held to discuss the problem and outline some action. Commander Garry presided. Also present were Lyons, O'Dwyer, Dowd, Garrett, and the two Sullivans. It was risky for top leaders to meet like this, but they had to risk it.

Their old nemesis Sergeant Roche, who defended the first barrack Lyons captured, was still operating from a very strongly fortified barrack. He had built up a group of spies to work for him. They included paid informers, unpaid informers, and unpaid ex-British officers who were retired and living in the Brigade area. The paid informers got £5 a week, good pay for the period and more if they came up with something really worthwhile.

The paid informers were low-lifes who would gladly sell their mothers. The other two types were strong farmers, usually Protestant and very happy with the Union. The last group, the officers hated and despised, the I.R.A. and called them "shinners" or ditch murderers. They all reported to Sergeant Roche whatever they could find.

The Sergeant rarely moved around the Brigade Area, and, if he did, it was always as part of a patrol of Tans or R.I.C. or army. Commander Garry said, "We will put him top of the list for execution, if we can find him. Can you help us with this?" he asked John O'Dowd.

"All I know is he goes to church on Sunday, being a good Catholic. The Tans drop him at the church gate and he walks around fifty yards along a path to the long aisle of the church. He is usually alone at this time. It is the only chance to get him."

"Nice intelligence work, John," said Garry. "But the parish priest would be furious with us, not to mention the bishop of the diocese. Headquarters in Dublin may not like it either, especially our defense minister Charlie Byrne."

"Don't worry about the parish priest," said Lyons. "He is a good friend of mine. I will smooth it over with him. It doesn't matter about the bishop. He is against us anyway. I can explain it to Mick Connor in Dublin. He knows about Roche too and wants him eliminated. He will explain it to Valero and the Cabinet."

"All right," Gary said. "So it is agreed that we will shoot him in the church grounds between the front gate and the porch door. One problem remains. Who will do the actual shooting? I would hate to order anyone for this. I will ask for volunteers." The Sullivans volunteered right away.

"I will do it," said James.

"And I will help him," added John.

Garry said, "Bring a gun in each hand, loaded and well tested beforehand. I don't want any mistakes. Make sure he is dead before ye leave. I will bring the rest of the flying column into the town. They will be near on hand to help ye if there is any problem."

The meeting broke up. For the next few days the column laid low. James and John practiced with their revolvers until the Commander was happy with their performance. Early on the following Sunday the column made its way to the town. They stayed out of sight in back yards and lanes until the Tans arrived at 10:45 for 11 A.M. Mass. They dropped Roche at the gate.

Two men with boxes in their hands stood at the gate collecting money. He threw a few pence in one box and began walking along the path to the porch. The Sullivans sneaked in behind him.

Nobody recognized them. Several late comers were hurrying in as well. Roche had almost reached the porch before they got an opening to shoot, making sure not to hit bystanders. They let him have it. James shot him in the head and John through the heart. He dropped dead on the spot.

Bystanders flung themselves on the ground and some of them ran away across the fields behind the church. The Sullivans ran out the front gate and rejoined the Flying Column. Garry ordered the column to march to billets ten miles away. There was intense activity by the British after the mass. They had suffered a serious reverse and gave the Sergeant a big funeral, forcing the local merchants to close their businesses as a token of respect.

The Brigade Council held another meeting to discuss further action against the spies. The head of the snake was gone, but there were more left to deal with. The bishop condemned the deed, but the parish priest was more guarded in his opinion.

Mick Connor was glad to hear of the removal of Roche. He never missed a chance to get inside the British lines. He had spies in Dublin Castle, even in their secret service and inside their army. He had managed to recruit the female secretary of General Kirkland who commanded the division that opposed Lyons' first brigade area. She had been married to an English major. They had a daughter. Trouble developed in the marriage and he absconded to England with the daughter. Mick Connor traced him to Liverpool and managed to get the daughter back to Ireland for the secretary. From then on she gave many a tip to the I.R.A.. They rented a house in the capital city of the county and if she had information she left it in a hiding place under the stairs, built by a carpenter. Everyday an I.R.A. courier checked for the papers, and if he found something sent it on to the Brigades.

In this way Garry found out there was a spy, or someone he suspected as a spy, in the third battalion area. This man had a code name "Aspen." That was all she could tell them, but the general placed a lot of importance on his reports.

"It is time we paid this man a call," said Lyons. John O'Dowd and his intelligence group had long suspected a strong farmer named Wood, a Protestant, but as yet had no proof of his guilt.

"Does he go to the barrack?" asked Garry.

"No I don't think so," said O'Dowd. "But maybe we could trick him into confessing. The British probably send someone every week to check for information. Maybe we could get someone to impersonate a British officer and call to see him."

"It is a long shot," said Lyons. "But worth a try if we can find somebody with a British accent."

"I know a man from Glasgow," said O'Dowd. "He joined the I.R.A. about six weeks ago. His parents were Irish born. His name is Doherty and he even wanted to join the Flying Column as he is an experienced soldier."

"We can ask him," said John Garry. "And if he agrees he can fight with the Column."

The next day O'Dowd contacted O'Doherty and he said he would help with the deception. O'Dowd brought him to meet the column commander, and he was impressed enough to accept him into the column.

A British army uniform, captured in a raid on a barrack, was given to him a few nights later and he marched with the column to the house of the suspect. The column waited nearby and Doherty knocked on the Protestant's door.

A maid opened the door. "There is a British officer here to see you, Mr. Wood."

"Send him in right away," replied Wood. They went into the parlour. He offered whiskey and tea to Doherty, but Doherty refused.

"I never drink on duty," he said. After some small talk they got down to business.

"Why did you not come out before this to see me? I was not able to make a report for three weeks because nobody came for it. I had important info. The Flying Column was here and visited nearby last week for several days. If ye had acted on my information they might all be dead now," said Wood.

Doherty apologized for the delay. He said they would be more prompt in future and send someone every week.

"You know I can't go to the barracks," said Wood.

"I know," said Doherty. He took out a notebook and said, "Give me as many names and addresses as you can and I will see to it that these ruffians are put behind bars."

"Better under the sod," said Wood. He read off a number of names from the local battalion.

"Do you know any of the Flying Column?" Doherty asked.

"I have heard the names, Lyons, Dwyer, and the Sullivan brothers. I can't say I could identify any of them but now you know who to look for."

"Do you know the leader?" asked Doherty. "He is a new man, not long with the column. Since he arrived, the whole Brigade has become really active. I hear he is a young, energetic type, a real thorn in our side. I don't know his name yet, but I'm working on it with some of my intelligence group."

"I need to visit them," said Doherty. "Can you give me some names and addresses?" He gave a few names but became a little suspicious of Doherty. He would not say any more so Doherty concluded it was time to call an end to the charade. He pulled his gun. "Put your hands up," he said and blew the whistle.

The spy put his hands up. In rushed Garry, Dwyer, Lyons, and the Sullivans.

"I would like to introduce John Garry the column commander and other important members." He showed the list of names to Garry. "By God," said Garry. "He really had all this battalion in his cross-hairs."

He pointed his gun at the spy. "You are sentenced to death for being a traitor to the Republic. You will be shot at dawn."

He refused any spiritual assistance. They took him away. A firing squad of six men shot him at dawn. They put a placard on his body saying, "spies and informers beware."

They used the body as bait to lure the British out, but they refused to take the bait and waited three days to remove the body.

They now had put a serious dent on the British spy group. They picked up and executed the spies Wood had mentioned. That left a few lesser spies. They captured one of the paid spies group. He gave up the names of colleagues in exchange for his life and was deported from the country. Some spies still existed in the brigade area but few were active now. There was a major drop in the casualty rate of the I.R.A.

The last spy they caught worked as a teacher in a national school. He used to drink in a local bar frequented by the Tans and R.I.C. He was suspected of spying but the I.R.A. had no proof. The Brigadier was very strict about proof and only accepted the death penalty for the most damning of evidence. Unfortunately some spies got away with it.

Two I.R.A. men were captured after they were betrayed to the Tans. The Tans picked out the exact house in the parish where they were hidden. They got the blame for shooting a judge.

The teacher had seen them enter the house and was the only one who knew they were there. The I.R.A. suspected the bar owner but he gave a good account of himself in the kangaroo court.

Besides he had put money into the I.R.A. fund. He gave up the teacher as the spy.

The captured I.R.A. men were treated horribly. They were kicked and beaten with rifle butts and pulled after lorries by the feet with their heads bouncing off the roads until dead. Their coffins were left open in the church for all to see. Everyone was shocked. The teacher was arrested by the I.R.A. and interrogated. Eventually he confessed. He tried to make excuses for himself. He said he just wanted the men arrested and not killed.

"Well they were murdered," said the column commander. "And in a repulsive manner. You will have to pay with your life." He sent for the parish priest to give him a chance for confession and communion. They shot him by firing squad. The really sad part of it was the spy had two brothers in the I.R.A..

The Brigade staff held another meeting to discuss the situation in the Brigade. They were all agreed that the spy situation was under control but there was another new menace on the horizon. The British would make a new, real push to smash the I.R.A. The new force would be called the Auxiliaries.

CHAPTER 8

THE AUXILIARIES

The British government recognized that they were not making progress in stamping out the I.R.A. by the middle of 1920. The R.I.C. was no longer the effective force it once was.

The Tans were little better than a rabble, sent in to help the R.I.C. The army was not having much success either. So they decided to recruit an elite force of ex-servicemen. Each one had to be a former officer with combat experience in the World War. Some had decorations up to and including the top British reward for bravery the Victoria Cross. This force was paid one pound a day, which in 1920 was excellent money. This was twice what the Tans got paid. Churchill was the main driving force behind the setting up of this force. They began arriving in Ireland in July 1920. They turned out to be the most ruthless force Ireland had seen for many a year.

They were organized in fifteen companies and scattered throughout Ireland, but most of them were sent to the southern counties. Their mission was to rub out the I.R.A. and terrorize the civilian population and force them not to help the I.R.A. volunteers. They dressed in a manner that could easily be mistaken for I.R.A. members, but they all had one distinctive item, the Glengarry cap. If you saw Glengarry caps you were dealing with the Auxiliaries.

They were armed to the teeth. Each one carried two revolvers in holsters strapped to their thighs, a Mills bomb bandolier of ammunition, Sam brown belt, and of course a Lee Enfield rifle.

They traveled around the country in fast moving lorries called Crossley Tenders. A couple of men rode in front and the rest sat on benches in the back of the lorry. The total number of this force was just short of fifteen hundred men. The British waged a propaganda campaign to promote the reputation of this force as super fighters and almost invincible. Their modus operandi was this:

They would arrive in a small town or village, roaring and shouting and firing shots in the air. They would order all the people out in the street for interrogation. No exceptions were allowed for old, young, or sick. It did not matter. Everyone was ordered out. If they didn't like the answers they got they would belt people with belts and with the butts of revolvers or rifles. They would hold the people hostage for hours until they were finished with their interrogation. They would take pot shots at farmers working in their fields. The farmers would run for cover as bullets flew all around them. If they were hit and killed, no questions would be asked.

They also did a lot of looting from all kinds of shops and didn't pay for drinks in the pubs. Their commander named Crozier tried to discipline them after they robbed a Unionist business in County Meath. He was sacked and the looters restored at their jobs. The British government was behind it all.

As the winter of 1920 approached no I.R.A. brigade had attacked the Auxies. This was bad for I.R.A. morale and for the morale of the people. Something would have to be done and soon.

Brigadier Lyons had not attacked them either, but he had an excuse of sorts. The Auxies invading his brigade area came from the next brigade area and moved in completely unpredictable routes. He would have to figure out where to attack them. He held a meeting to discuss the matter. John Garry, Dwyer, the Sullivans, Garrett, O'Dowd, several battalion commanders, and himself were present.

"O'Dowd," he asked. "Have you studied the movements of the Auxies? What have you for us?"

O'Dowd said, "They come into our area and when they come to the nearest cross roads they go either south, east, or west, usually in two lorries but sometimes three. The only chance of meeting them is before they come to the cross roads, a stretch of road for a few hundred yards. Unfortunately this is not the best ambush country."

Garry and Lyons said they would go and check it out and decide what to do. The next day they went in a pony and trap to the site. There was a lack of roadside ditches and very few fields. It was mostly Bogland with a few small paths used by the farmers to save and bring home their turf. It would be hard if not impossible to retreat from there if things went wrong howev,er they decided to go ahead with it. There were two rocky outcrops which would be the only cover they could use on the eastern side of the north-south running stretch of road. At the southern end of this stretch of road was a small side road and a very low stone wall, which would provide some cover. There was only one house visible, a hundred yards along the side road. The farmer was building a stone outhouse and the farmer had some stones there ready for the stone mason. They could take some stones from the farmer and raise the wall's height, enough to give cover.

He could take them back after the ambush. Brigadier Lyons and Commander Garry decided to bring forty men together for a week's training about ten miles away. The best men they could find would be chosen to fight this important fight. The training camp ended on a Saturday night in November. The men were told what the objective was and a priest was called to hear confessions. This time they skipped individual confessions in favour of a general confession. The men formed four rows, contemplated in silence their sins and said an act of contrition. They all got absolution. The priest then said mass and every man was then ready to meet his maker.

John Gary stood before the men and gave a short speech.

"We are going into action tomorrow against the Auxiliaries. Ye all know who they are and what they are doing in Ireland. We must fight and defeat them. It is important not only for our Brigade but for all the brigades in Ireland. They are killers without mercy. There will be no retreat. We either wipe them out or they wipe us out. See to it that those terrorists are the ones lying dead tomorrow. Get a few hours sleep. Ye will have to get up about 3 A.M. and march ten miles to Ballymartin the ambush site. We will move under cover of darkness and be in ambush positions about 8 A.M.." With that he dismissed them all and they went to their billets.

They were all out of bed by 3 A.M. and soon were on the march. For some of the way they used main roads but mostly side roads and where necessary across fields and bogs and streams, small hills, and valleys. They reached the ambush site and were all deployed by 9 A.M.

Garry picked three men to take up a position behind the stone wall. There was not much cover there, but it would have to do after it was raised a little by some extra stones. The three men he picked were Daffy, Duffy, and Kerrigan.

These men had been recommended by the 5th battalion leader because of their experience and fighting record. They had taken part in several important fights against coastguard stations and barracks in their battalion area. They were all good shots and quick on the draw. The attack would be started from here when the leading lorry reached this position.

Section one of ten men he placed ten yards to the north behind a rocky outcrop. This section under James Sullivan would attack the first lorry as soon as the command post opened fire.

Section two under Brigadier Lyons was placed north of number one section but nearer to a bend on the road. This section would attack the second lorry expected. Ten experienced fighters made up this group. Section three also made up of ten men were placed fifty yards north of the bend with a view of the road. This group would act as a flanking group and could fire on a third lorry if it came and also help attack the second lorry if not needed for a third lorry. They were on a small hill with a view of the approach road and were under the command of John Dwyer. All the sections were east of the road.

The fourth and last section of six men, under John Sullivan, were placed west of the road, behind a rocky outcrop. Their job was to keep the Auxies from escaping to the west and taking up fighting positions there. Forty men in all would take part in the ambush. Garry knew he could rely on his veteran commanders to stand and fight. Nobody would turn tail and run.

It was winter and cold, damp and miserable. A shower of rain came to add to the misery.

They had no food or drink. All they could do was lie there, shiver, and wait for the Auxies. They could come any time or maybe not at all. Too many times successive columns had waited in vain for the British and had to march away frustrated. Hour after hour passed until 3 P.M. when a scout signaled the approach of the enemy. Commander Garry gave the order, "Lie flat until I blow my whistle. Pass it along."

Every man pressed close to the ground. Two lorries came into the ambush position at a fairly fast speed, and about fifty yards apart. As the leading lorry came within twenty yards of the stone wall, Garry's group opened fire, while he himself hurled a Mills bomb and blew his whistle. The grenade exploded in the cab killing both the driver and the man beside him.

Section one opened fire. The lorry came on until it stopped five yards from the stone wall.

The Auxies in the back of the lorry jumped off three of them, lied down to fire back at number one section, and four more rushed at the stone wall group. The fighting became hand to hand.

The Garry group drove their bayonets into the Auxies and Garry fired his parabellum at the three lying down. After five minutes all the Auxies in the first lorry were dead.

Meanwhile the second lorry was stopped near Lyon's section. Most of them had survived the first volley and fought back with determination. Garry brought his men and five from section one to attack them from the rear. After ten minutes the Auxies had lost half their number and cries of surrender were heard.

"Pour the lead into them," ordered Garry. The I.R.A. fired at them until they all died.

A third lorry had arrived but stopped one hundred yards from the bend, when they heard the firing in front. Some of them crossed into a field north of the road but Dwyer's group drove them back to the road, inflicting casualties. A few more tried to get into positions south of the road, but John Sullivan's group drove them back with a withering fire. The Auxies had seen enough and decided to retreat and seek help. They managed to reverse to an opening and turn the lorry. They headed back to their barracks about ten miles away.

Garry brought his men together near the second lorry. They collected the rifles, ammunition, and papers of the Auxies and set fire to the lorries. Garry spoke a few words to them, praising all the participants and thanking them for their efforts.

"This ambush will be remembered long after we are all dead. It will make the British government sit up and think the I.R.A. are no push-overs. We must get out of here right away in case the enemy comes back. We will march ten miles to specially prepared billets."

They set off right away. The ammunition was distributed and some men had to carry a captured rifle as well as his own. However, it was a welcome burden. Twenty new rifles would be added to the brigade armament. They reached their billets about 11 P.M.. The men were tired, wet, hungry, and nearly exhausted. The local company had a cottage ready to house the men for the night, and women prepared food and drink for them. They remained there for a few days until it was safer to disperse. The British scoured the countryside for them to no avail.

The British government was furious over the loss. Their best troops were smashed. The super fighters had been badly beaten. This group would no longer be the great terrorists they had been for months. From now on they would be a lot more careful in their dealings with the I.R.A.

The British destroyed several houses, shops and haybarns in the area near the ambush.

They posted notices that anyone walking with their hands in their pockets would be shot at sight.

They claimed the I.R.A. used hatchets on the bodies of the Auxies but that was a lie. No corpse was interfered with. They admitted that twenty auxiliaries were killed. "Those fellows will not bother us anymore," said Garry. Christmas was near and it was time for a break.

CHAPTER 9

CHRISTMAS BREAK

As Christmas approached in 1920 it was time to take a rest from guerilla war. The column had zig-zagged its way around the brigade area, but no clash with British forces occurred.

Commandant Garry decided to disband the column and wait for January to renew the war. There was some talk of peace but nobody believed in that. Most of the column could go home to their own parishes, but some would have to stay on the run. The British were trying very hard to establish a new intelligence system and the homes of known suspects were watched closely. The year 1920 had been a great year for the I.R.A. They had gone from strength to strength. More men then they could ever arm came forward to join the I.R.A..

The Sullivan brothers paid a short visit to their parents' house. They arrived early Christmas day but left in the afternoon again and cycled ten miles away to the home of a great supporter called Mrs. Tobin. They arrived about 7 P.M. She had great welcome for them and immediately prepared a meal for them. She had some goose left over and plenty of sweet cake and some stronger refreshment as well. They enjoyed the meal and after it sat by the fire. A lively conversation developed. She wanted to hear every detail of the actions they had taken part in.

She was particularly interested in the R.I.C. being put under pressure. She was a woman of about fifty with a long memory. She remembered the Land league struggle against the landlords and had seen families thrown out on the roadside. She knew older people who had lived through the famine years of 1845 to 1847. Her father, an old man and Fenian of over eighty years who lived with them, also joined in to tell stories of the Fenian movement. "We were destroyed by poor leadership and informers, but I think this generation will succeed where we failed," he said.

"Ye handed on the tradition of resistance to us," James said. "And in that sense ye didn't fail at all." That pleased the old man as he took a puff of his pipe.

At nine o'clock they all got on their knees for the Rosary. Mrs. Tobin called out the prayers and the rest responded. The flag floor was hard on the knees and the sugan chair hard on elbows but they suffered through it. After the fifth decade came the trimmings, and the aid of several saints was invoked. Then to end it all she prayed for the souls in Purgatory. Then the Rosary ended and everyone got up and sat on their chairs again. The old man said, "I hope they are letting some of the souls in Purgatory out or there will be no room for me when I get there and they might send me to hell." He had a skeptical streak and had no love for the bishops who condemned the Fenians to hell. Everybody laughed at the idea of the overcrowding in Purgatory.

Mrs. Tobin made some more tea. The lively conversation resumed and the night passed quickly. It was 11 pm and time for bed. Mrs. Tobin had never been raided and it was considered a safe house to stay in, if you could call any house safe anymore. It was Christmas and surely the British would take a break.

Suddenly they heard the sound of a lorry and the dogs barked ferociously as the Tans dismounted and ran towards the front door. "Out, quick, use the backdoor!" Mrs. Tobin shouted to the Sullivans as they were just about to go upstairs to bed. "I will try and stall them if I can," she said. They grabbed their overcoats and revolvers and dashed out the back.

The Tans didn't have enough time to block off the back escape route so the Sullivans made a run for it along a small field. They scrambled over a wall into the next field as a powerful searchlight was concentrated on the wall. The Tans fired a volley after them but they had the cover of the wall. Then they moved to the left over another wall, then turned right and ran down a slope towards a river. They could hear the Tans closing in on them and cursing as they sought their prey. The river was wide and deep. They could not wade across, or swim. The water was about four feet deep near the bank, so they jumped in and ducked under the water and sucked air through reeds. They could hear the Tans looking for them. Their leader could not understand where they had gone and called off the search and headed back to the house.

They interrogated Mrs. Tobin. She claimed that the men were neighbours who were just visiting and panicked as they should be in their own homes according to British regulations. "Go and check for yourselves," she said and told them where the house was. She was only playing for time so the Sullivans could escape. The Lieutenant asked her if she knew the Sullivan brothers.

She replied, "No, I never heard of them." Then she realized that they must have been acting on a tip off. Why did they come directly to her house on Christmas night?

Meanwhile the Sullivans got out of the river. It had been a nightmare time under the water.

"What can we do now?" John asked.

James said, "I believe there is a house about half a mile away near the river bank. We can go there and see if they have a boat and borrow it to cross the river.

"Why not try a bridge?" asked John.

"No," said James. "They will watch the bridges. We must cross the river. There are some good safe houses on the other side.

There were some loyalist houses on this side of the river, but they don't know which was which. They walked along the bank until they came to a house and knocked on the door. The owner opened the door. They introduced themselves as men from the I.R.A. who wanted to borrow a boat to cross the river. The man was a loyalist, but he had seen a neighbor shot as an informer so he was careful to mind his own business. He had land at the other side of the river and used his boat regularly as a shortcut to go and check on his cattle. The last people he wanted to see were I.R.A. men.

James said, "If you are a loyalist, we will tell our Brigadier you helped us and you will be compensated for the use of your boat from the I.R.A. fund." The loyalist had heard some bad stories about the I.R.A. Mostly lying British propaganda. He was astonished at the politeness and civility of these young men. He decided to help them.

"I will take ye across the river myself," he said.

"Thank you," they said. "We will make sure our Brigadier knows about you and you will never be troubled for the rest of this war." He took them across the river in his boat. They knew a safe house and knocked on the door. The door was opened and to their surprise they found Garry and Lyons there.

They thought they were seeing ghosts at first, with these two men arriving in the middle of the night so they all sat down to hear their story.

"We were in Tobin's house," said James. "And there was a sudden raid. We were lucky to make an escape out the back door. A loyalist helped us and ferried us across the river."

"A loyalist?" said the Brigadier. "That is unusual. We will never bother that man again for the rest of the war. Most of them have no time for us but if they stay neutral we will leave them alone."

"Did anyone see ye go into that house?" asked Garry. They tried to think back and remembered something.

"A man went by on a bicycle and saluted us just as we turned into the by-road leading to Tobin's house. We saw him enter a house about one hundred yards away further up the road. We thought no more about it until ye asked us."

"We will have O'Dowd work on this right away. We could have an informer on our hands," said Garry.

The next day O'Dowd sent one of his intelligence staff to question Mrs. Tobin. She explained how the Tans asked for the Sullivans and nobody else. She got the impression they were acting on a definite tip. He went back and reported this to the Brigadier.

"Go back he said and tell Mrs. Tobin about the character the Sullivans saw on the bicycle and ask her does she know who this is." He did this next day and Mrs. Tobin said that this man was the local postman. He would know who lived in every house on his route and especially if any strangers entered the house.

The postman was arrested the next day by the local company and brought to a kangaroo court presided over by John Garry. The Sullivans confirmed he was the man they saw on Christmas Day. He protested his innocence. Some members of the local company had long suspected this man. He was often out at night when nobody else was out. If anyone saw him, he would say he was looking for his donkey that broke out of his field and wandered onto the main road.

"I'm in two minds about you," said Garry. "If it was you who spied, you are lucky no I.R.A. man was killed. If anyone was killed, you would be facing a firing squad. We are not killers and hate to wrong anybody. So I strongly suggest you leave the country as soon as possible." The postman was greatly relieved at being allowed to go and thanked the court for its clemency and headed for his home.

"We should have plugged him," said James Sullivan. "I would bet the farm he was a spy."

"We will soon see, after what the British do in the next few days if he is a spy or not," said Brigadier Lyons.

The next day a British lorry stopped at his house and took him away to the barracks and evacuated him to England soon after. "I told ye so," said James Sullivan.

"Well he will never bother us again," said Garry.

CHAPTER 10

ATTEMPT AT ENCIRCLEMENT

By the middle of January 1921 the orders were out to the Flying Column to assemble again. It would consist of some former members but also some new men. The members had not been idle during the lay-off. They took part in trenching work and damaging bridges and branch railway lines. Some also took shots at barracks all around the brigade area. This made it hard for the British forces to move around. They had to be constantly on the alert never knowing when an attack might come. Often the phone lines would be cut and they had to just sit there waiting for an attack until daylight came. It was nerve wracking.

They now started to move about in larger convoys of three or four lorries, mostly armor plated. The barracks were fortified with sandbags, and barbed wire and loopholes enabled them to fire out on all sides. I.R.A. attacks on barracks were not as frequent now and similarly with ambushes. The Flying Column had to be increased in number to over one hundred men.

This was a difficult task for the Commander to move his men around the Brigade area, feed them, and find billets for them. However, there was no other choice if the war was to be continued. They lay in ambush several times at different places during the rest of January and all through February but nothing happened. The column Commander suspected that spies were in action again but he had no proof. Several times they waited all day in ambush to no avail.

March arrived, cold and windy but with some good days as well. They had information from their own intelligence service that the Sussex regiment would travel between a certain two towns. He prepared an ambush for them but they never came. He learned that the Sussex learned of the ambush and did not travel. Instead they contacted General Kirkland, saying they had pinpointed the location of the column. The general decided to launch a major encirclement to try and annihilate the column. He took his map and put his finger on the spot where he figured the column was. He looked around at the towns north, south, west, and east of this spot. Every town had garrisons of troops and he ordered all to converge on the area where the column was, starting that day and all through the night. The general's secretary, still working for the I.R.A., sent the information right away to John O'Dowd, Brigade chief of intelligence. Immediately he headed to find the column and let them know of the grave danger to the column.

Garry had moved his men some miles north of where they lay in ambush for the Sussex.

This was a piece of luck for the column and would mean the British were not focused on the exact spot. O'Dowd found them over six miles north of where they lay in ambush on the tenth of March. It was now the evening of the eleventh when O'Dowd arrived at Garry's headquarters.

They held a quick Council of War: Garry, Lyons, O'Dwyer, the Sullivan brothers and all the section Commanders. They listened to O'Dowd's information.

"This is the toughest situation we have faced so far," said Lyons. "What can we do?" he asked Garry.

"I don't think we can slip through their lines. They would have all the advantages, as they are coming across fields as well as along the roads in lorries. They could hold the high ground and mow us down at will. It is better if we wait for them to come here and attack them piecemeal. That is our only hope. They can't time the encirclement to get here at the same time so whichever group comes first we will attack them with a sudden ambush that will take them by surprise."

The men all went to bed early that night about 10 P.M.. They needed a good rest to be ready for the battle next day. Scouts from the local company were sent out in all directions to watch for the approach of the British groups. The lights of their lorries were visible in several directions but it became obvious that a group of over three hundred would get to the ambush positions of Ballybrickan first. They were coming from the west along a long fairly straight road, from a town about six miles away. They seemed to stop and start. Some troops moved along the fields on either side of the road, while others stayed on the lorries. They raided any houses they could find in search of the I.R.A.

The scouts rushed in to the billet where Garry and his officers were. They got out of bed right away. The scout informed him of the situation. He immediately decided to assemble the column and set an ambush inside a wall on the main road. It was still dark, but he figured it would be daylight when the British reached the ambush position. In a half hour all the men were assembled in a field near the road. He explained the position to them and ordered each section commander to lead his men to positions he would decide on.

He had a total of 120 men under his command. He divided them into eight sections of fifteen. Section one under John Dwyer took the position on the right flank on high ground. He could fire on the approach road for hundreds of yards and stop any troops coming across country away from their lorries.

Daffy, Duffy, and Kerrigan were in charge of sections two, three, and four and placed inside the wall on the northern side of the road. These were veterans of the auxie ambush and held in high regard by the column commander.

He took up a position about halfway between the western section two and the eastern section five. He was joined by O'Dowd, and both carried parabellums.

Section number five under John Sullivan was on the extreme left with a view of the road to the east. Brigadier Lyons was placed one hundred yards farther north, opposite a small stream. He had a good view of the countryside to the east and northeast. He was behind a wall on higher ground. He led section six.

James Sullivan lead section seven to protect the rear and to stop any troops coming from the north. He was also on high ground and behind a wall.

The last section, eight, was in position one hundred yards north of section one, under Garrett. He was expected to be flexible and deploy his men in whatever direction he saw fit. No section was allowed to move without instructions from Garry as the British were coming from all directions.

Some scouts had already joined the column from the west and would act as runners, to keep the sections in touch and help to carry captured equipment if needed. By 7 A.M. all were ready to stand up to Ireland's old enemy of seven hundred years.

By 9 A.M. the approach of the British was signaled. The lorries came on slowly to the position. All the sections were north of the road. Every man lay low pressed hard into the ground. No firing was allowed until the first lorry reached John Sullivan's section five at the eastern end. When the first of twenty lorries reached this position he opened fire and shot the driver. The lorry stopped and all the other sections opened fire at once.

The men were armed with Lee Enfield rifles, one of the best rifles ever. Five bullets could be fired so quickly that it seemed like machine-gun fire. They poured lead into the ten lorries that came into the ambush position. The range was only ten yards and the casualty list was very high. Any soldier not killed or wounded jumped off the lorry and retreated towards the south. Section one under Dwyer blazed away at the nearmost lorries and Garrett's men shot several troops who moved north on a by-road trying to outflank Dwyer. They soon retreated to the safety of their lorries. They all had seen enough, and the lorries turned around on the road and retreated.

Garry ordered his men out on the road and fired several volleys at the retreating British, south of the road. They failed to regroup and launch another attack. Garry could hardly believe his eyes. They had repulsed a force of three hundred men. He ordered the ammunition collected and any guns lying around. The ammunition was distributed among the men, who were now well armed and ready for more battle.

John Sullivan came to Garry with a peculiar looking weapon under his arm. Garry recognized the weapon as a Lewis gun, one of the best machine guns of World War I.

"I found this near the first lorry," said John. There was a peculiar looking circular thing on top of it.

"That is the ammunition pan," said Garry. "Go back to the lorry and look for more." He went back right away and found ten pans of ammunition. A man in John's section said he could use it, as he had served in France with the American army. He was given the gun right away.

Right then another British force was approaching a half-mile away from the east and southeast. Garry could have avoided action but the morale of the men was higher and the addition of the machine gun boosted confidence. The lorries came along slowly on the main road and troops on foot mainly across fields north of the road.

He re-deployed his men quickly moving sections two, three, and four to reinforce John Sullivan and Lyons. Section four was now south of the road with a good field of fire, and sections two and three on either side of Lyons. The men held their fire until the British were fifty yards away coming up a slope. Then Garry opened fire and O'Brien with the Lewis gun mowed down so many of them that the rest turned and fled. They ran to their lorries and turned tail and ran. Garry and his men collected the guns and ammunition. The local company arrived with petrol and paraffin oil to burn the abandoned lorries. Now Garry had plenty options. He could retreat to the south, east, or west, but nobody wanted to retreat. More British were coming in from the north, but now the I.R.A. was better armed. They had thousands of rounds of ammunition and of course the machine gun. No, they would not retreat. They would repel the British force coming from the north.

Firing broke out at James Sullivan's section and James and his men were trying to repel a strong force of several hundred men. They inflicted lots of casualities but lost a few of their own.

Garry moved Lyons, Daffy, and Duffy and their sections to help James. They shot a major who was urging his men forward, and this seemed to knock the heart out of the British and they retreated leaving many men dead on the field and more wounded.

A smaller group came in from the northwest, but they were met by Garrett's number eight section. Garry was able to move more men to help Garrett and after fifteen minutes, these British troops also retreated and returned to barracks. Now the way was open to the I.R.A. to retreat towards the west. A great victory had been won by 122 men against a force of at least one thousand men.

Garry called in his flankers Dwyer, John Sullivan, and Kerrigan and they formed up in sections around the column commander. He made a short speech, congratulating his men on their success. They collected the bodies of five dead comrades and left them in an outhouse to be moved later by the local company to a place of burial.

"We will leave here in a westerly direction," said Garry. "I don't expect to meet any more British forces, but we are not sure, of course. We have a few wounded men, but they can march with us. Several men will have to carry an extra rifle, at least as far as the next parish, where they can be hidden in dumps by the company in that parish."

"Section leader Duffy with his men will lead us out of here as he is a local man with detailed knowledge of the countryside. Some of his unit will travel on both sides of the road in fields to prevent an ambush by the British. Food will be provided in the next parish, where we will make a short halt. Then we will march on to billets about thirty miles west of here, where food and drink will be provided by the local company and Cumann Na Mban girls. John Sullivan and his section will bring up the rear so once again, thanks to everybody, and let the march begin."

So they zig-zagged across the country, mostly on side roads, across fields, over hedges, across small streams and small rivers, and through some woods and bogs. The food in the first halting place was a relief to starving men. They never tasted food so good.

Everyone was dead tired after the recent hectic days of waiting in ambush, then marching to Ballybrickan not getting much sleep and the hectic battle against superior British forces. The battle had taken about two hours and it was late in the day about 8 P.M. when they reached the pre-arranged billets. At one point they saw some troops in the distance but they didn't interfere. The men retired early that night, guarded by the local company.

CHAPTER 11

ATTACK ON BARRACKS OF BALLYBOW

After the battle of Ballybrickan the British government indulged in their usual lies about what really happened. They had lost at least about one hundred men, but they admitted only ten dead and five wounded. Besides, they claimed, the I.R.A. lost fifty men and seventy wounded. To excuse their failures they claimed about five hundred men fought on the I.R.A. side with rifles, revolvers, machine guns, grenades, and loads of ammunition. They had probably begun to believe their own lies.

However, some of the more thoughtful among their military leadership began to worry, especially Sir Henry Wilson, Chief of Staff of the army. They began to think they could not win a military victory without flooding the country with troops. Where would they come from? The English public had enough of war. Troops would have to be withdrawn from other parts of the empire with the resulting weakening effect. They informed Lloyd George, who began to realize it would take political and diplomatic skill to get England out of this corner.

Commandant Garry and his men were well armed now and morale was high. They would carry on the war in their brigade until told to stop by the G.H.Q.

For some time they lay in ambush in several places, but no engagement occurred. There was a certain barracks that was a thorn on their side. If they could capture it an area of about 250 square miles would be free of enemy garrisons. Then the nearest garrisons would be twenty miles away. Travel was difficult for the British, and to capture the barrack would give the I.R.A. a large area for rest and recuperation. Harassment by this garrison would end.

The barracks was located at Ballybow about a mile from the sea, which lay on its south side. A long east-west road ran through the town. Another north-south running road divided into two different directions to its northwest and northeast just north of the town. The building was a two-story structure, completely detached on the eastern edge of the town. A few houses lay across the road and open fields to the east and south. There was a wall parallel to the barracks at the back which would give cover. There was no hope of an attack through the roof now as the building was detached and had sandbags and barbed wire all around, so ladders could not be used. The only opening was a path to the front door between the barbed wire.

Garry ordered his intelligence officer O'Dowd to look into the movements of the garrison and its numerical strength. To get to the door, he found you would have to open a door at the beginning of the path with a latch. The local I.O. watched it carefully for weeks and discovered that it was usually left unlocked.

The garrison had grown careless and indeed had bragged that their post could not be captured. They were right, up to this point the brigade did not have anything that would blow a hole in the wall to allow access to the barracks. They had begged headquarters for an expert in mine making, and at the beginning of March, such an expert arrived in the brigade area.

A substance called chlorate of potash was needed to construct the mine. It could be bought in small quantities. Brigadier Lyons ordered each company to buy a few ounces of the stuff at the time. By the middle of April, a good size mine was ready for use.

The column commander set a date for the attack on the barracks for April 15th at 1 A.M.

The mine was very heavy. It was encased in a wooden box and looked more like a coffin than anything else. Four men were needed to carry it on their shoulders. The mine was carried on a common horse-drawn cart to a house a mile from the barracks on the 14th. This house was owned by a sympathizer of the I.R.A. Garry had to pick four men to carry the mine, each about 5'9" to make it easy to balance.

They practiced carrying the mine to the door of an outhouse. The I.R.A. formed two lines at right angles to the door and with a space between the lines, the same width as the path between the barbed wire at the barracks. After two hours of this Garry was satisfied they could do it without getting caught in the barbed wire.

He picked four cool and brave veteran fighters to carry the mine, namely the two Sullivans and Daffy and Duffy. Kerrigan was given the job of lighting the fuse which would dangle from the back of the box. They would have seven minutes to get out to safety after the fuse was lit. A column of fifty men were assembled that evening and told of the coming attack. The local company would provide road blocks and scouts. Garry estimated they would be against at least twenty-five R.I.C. and Tans but no one knew for sure. They could have machine guns and loads of grenades. The column was billeted locally that night and kept a low profile next day before the attack. The mine was brought by horse and cart to a house across the road from the barracks.

Garry deployed his men as follows: (1) Ten men under himself to storm the barracks. (2) Ten men under Garrett to collect the arms. (3) Ten men under O'Leary to burn down the building. (4) Ten men under Lyons in the houses opposite. (5) Ten men under Dwyer behind the house.

Timing would be very important. The road block men would start trenching and cutting trees at 10 P.M. The phone and telegraph system would be knocked out five minutes before the attack, and at 1 A.M. exactly the mine would be carried to the door and the fuse lit.

Everybody was in position and ready before 1 A.M.. They removed their boots and had noiselessly entered the town. There was no response from the barrack. The mine carriers lifted their mine and crossed the road. Garry opened the latch and door to the path and the four carriers carried it in and left it down carefully against the barrack door. They had left their overcoats across the road, so as not to get caught in the barbed wire. Kerrigan lit the fuse and they all walked across the road and lay flat. There was a great explosion. The door was blown in. A big breach was made and all the windows in the front were blown away.

The I.R.A. brought several sticks with them, and wrapped sacking around the sticks and soaked the sacking with paraffin and petrol from tins. When lit they hurled them into the barracks, through the breach and windows.

The explosion aroused the garrison and they fought back right away, hurling out grenades and firing their rifles. The I.R.A. threw in grenades and canister rounds. Every time a grenade exploded, the I.R.A. nearby lay flat and the fragments flew harmlessly upwards.

After fifteen minutes Garry was able to lead his group of ten into the building as the firing from the lower floor faded away. A few R.I.C. were already dead and their bodies were consumed by the spreading fire. Most of the R.I.C. were upstairs. Lyons in front and Dwyer behind kept up rapid fire and prevented their escape.

Garrett brought his group in to collect any arms but they only found a few rifles and two boxes of ammunition. Most of the weapons were upstairs. They all began firing their rifles and revolvers through the ceiling to try and bring it down but to no avail.

There was a stairway that led to the top floor, but it was impossible to go up there because of heavy fire by the R.I.C. After a while the stairs caught fire and could no longer be used. The R.I.C. fought on until their ammunition was gone and all their grenades thrown. Then they asked to surrender and Garry agreed. He was angry he would not capture more weapons and ammunition but he gave them quarter. This garrison had behaved well and didn't commit any atrocities. They threw their rifles into the blazing stairs and scrambled down a rope from a back window, towards the east of the house. They were nearly all wounded. They were herded across the road to a school for shelter and medical treatment.

Garry gathered his men together and made a short address. He thanked every man for his part in the success. He made a special mention of the men who carried in the mine to the barrack door. He only wished there was a reward like the Victoria Cross, he could give them. The men were tired and disheveled and had blackened faces after fighting inside the building.

The group under O'Leary had made sure to burn the building before they left the town, so that it became a complete wreck and could no longer be used by the enemy. Two local men were detailed to guard the R.I.C. and Tans as the column withdrew. They pretended to march east at first then wheeled north about a mile east of the town, to reach billets ten miles away by early afternoon.

CHAPTER 12

DUBLIN CALLS

In May 1921 Brigadier Lyons got an important dispatch from G.H.Q. in Dublin. "Mr. Valero would like to see you," it said. "He wants to know the position of the I.R.A. at this point of the struggle and what are its chances of success."

They held a brigade council meeting to discuss this development. Somebody would have to go to Dublin to discuss the situation with the President of the Sinn Fein government, but who? Nobody was anxious to leave the brigade. It was too long of a journey on foot. A motor car trip was out of the question as the British stopped and searched every car on the road. They could cycle, but that was a bit far as well and also bicycles were stopped regularly. That left only a train journey.

"You should go," John Garry said to Liam Lyons. "You have been to Dublin a few times and Mick Connor knows you. It would be a break for you from the hardship of leading the brigade." After pondering it over for a while he agreed.

"I would like to bring the Sullivan brothers with me as body-guards. They could use a break as well." John Garry agreed with reluctance. He would stay with the Flying Column and move into the area of the brigade just cleared of the enemy after the destruction of Ballybow barracks.

Mick Connor warned them not to carry guns. If caught with a gun at this point in the war, it meant death by firing squad or hanging. They would have to create false identities and pretend they had nothing to do with I.R.A. activity. Lyons decided to travel as a commercial traveller for a candle making company and the Sullivans posed as engineering students. There were some engineering students in the column who coached the Sullivans and gave them some books to read a week before the departure date. They felt confident they could bluff their way. Lyons got some paraphernalia from a real commercial traveler and a loan of his identity as well. The Sullivans also assumed false names. By mid-May they were ready and headed for Dublin by train.

They were all dressed in new suits, shirts, socks, shoes, and overcoats. They put aside their leggings and trench coats. All of these were paid for from the brigade fund. They entered the train and were on the move by 9 A.M.. They took a compartment together but, just before they left, an Englishman came and took a seat with them. He was a soldier going on leave. At first they ignored him and read their anti-Irish newspapers but after an hour he began to speak. They figured that he didn't know any of them.

"These are awful times we live in," he said. "I'm so sick of this war. I never expected any of it after being in the trenches in France. I could get no work so I ended up here. I hope it ends soon."

"We are all tired of it," said Liam Lyons. "I blame the stupid politicians. They should never have allowed it to come to this."

"Do you think ye can beat the rebels?" asked James Sullivan.

"We are mostly in the dark," replied the soldier, "going on wild goose chases and arresting men who often turn out to be harmless. I think we should pull out altogether." The I.R.A. men could barely resist laughing but they kept straight faces. Soon they reached Kingsbridge Station and got off the train. They said goodbye to the English soldier and wished him a happy holiday.

There were British secret service men on the platform scouring the passengers, on the look-out for I.R.A. men coming to the city. They didn't spot Lyons and the Sullivans and the three got in a taxi outside the station.

"Take us to Irwin's Pub, Parnell Street," asked Liam Lyons. He did and they arrived in half an hour. The bar-man gave a code word donkey and they had the right answer grey.

"Ye can go up stairs. A man will meet ye up there in a short time," he said.

As they waited up there a tall, well-built man over six feet tall and sixteen stone weight, exploded into the room. This was the famous Mick Connor.

"It is great to see you again, Liam," he said.

"These are the Sullivan brothers, James and John," said Liam. And to the Sullivan brothers he said, "This is Mick Connor." They all shook hands and Mick ordered a round of drinks from down stairs which the barman brought up on a tray.

"I hope ye had an uneventful trip coming here," he said. They told him about the British soldier. He laughed and said "I have to socialize with them myself sometimes as part of my intelligence work. I have often drank with English secret service men. Of course they don't know me, but if they did I would be in jail long ago. There was a price of $10,000 on his head but so far nobody had succeeded in earning it."

"What can ye tell me about the brigade? I know ye have had great success but can ye keep it going, and for how long?"

"Nobody can really answer that" said Liam. "We are ready to fight on, but we have a chronic lack of arms and ammunitions. We have plenty of men ready to fight but no arms for them. We need machine guns, grenades, material for mines, and above all .303 ammunition for the Flying Column."

Mick was well aware of all this. Every day he got requests from all over Ireland for arms and ammunition, but he could not supply a trickle of what was needed.

"I will let ye in on a top secret project I have under way. I have ordered a shipload of stuff from Italy and I expect it in a month. I hope to land it in your brigade area, as ye have access to the coast. When ye return to the brigade, I want ye to make plans to land the arms, hide the stuff, and distribute it among the neighbouring brigade. Of course ye will get a considerable portion of it for the first brigade."

The Sullivans were delighted to hear this but Lyons was a bit worried. "Don't you think, Mick, he asked. "That a quiet area with less British forces than the first brigade would be better?"

"No, I don't," he replied. "Some of these areas have been useless and done little or no fighting. I can't trust them to do a good job in landing the arms."

"Well thanks, Mick, for thinking so highly of us" said Liam. "We will get moving on it right away." With that, Mick concluded the meeting.

He took them for a lunch in Sackville Street and after that they headed for Valero's office in Merrion Square.

As they went along Dolier Street they were stopped by a patrol of Auxies. The three countrymen were ill at ease, not having met any Auxies since they ambushed them in their brigade area.

"Keep cool," said Mick and he walked up to the major in charge. The three others were ordered to put their hands up and stand against the wall to be searched. Mick approached the major, took out a package of cigarettes, and offered him one.

"Are those rebels at it again, major?" he asked.

"Yes," said the major. "There was an ambush in Camden Street an hour ago and we are looking for the culprits."

"I'm sorry to hear this," said Mick. "These rebels made our lives a misery. I can't even take my friends for lunch without having the heart put crossways in me."

"We are only doing our duty," replied the major.

"I'm glad ye are" said Mick. The sergeant had finished his search.

"They are all clean, major," he said.

"Ye can pass through" said the major.

They did not need to be told a second time.

When they were out of sight of the Auxies Mick laughed heartily, but Brigadier Lyons was annoyed. "Why didn't you send a scout ahead? We could all have been captured. We have no desire to wind up on the end of a rope and that is certainly what would be our fate if captured and identified."

Mick became serious. "I have to suppress the idea of being chased all the time. I go around as if I have a right to do so. I hide out in the open. They have no decent photograph of me and I have eliminated a lot of their best agents. They probably think I hide in a dugout in Wicklow or that I have members of my squad with me all the time. I don't do this or even carry a gun. I pose as an ordinary businessman and it has worked for me so far. My only real danger is to be betrayed from inside."

"I'm glad it has worked for you," said Brigadier Lyons, "and that you can continue to avoid capture. You have done great work for the cause." By now they had reached Merrion Square where Valero had an office. He no longer stayed at his home in Greystones. His hiding place was known only to a few. Connor knocked on the door. A secretary opened it and led them into a room, used as an office by the President.

He introduced Brigadier Lyons and the Sullivans and then took his leave as he had other matters to attend to. Valero got up from his desk and shook hands with all three. They all knew and admired his fighting record. He had been the most successful commandant in the 1916 rebellion. His command of Boland Mills had inflicted more casualties on the British than any other leader. He had been elected President of Sinn Fein and the Volunteers in 1917. He had toured America to spread the word about Ireland's quest for freedom and he had collected a lot of money to run the underground Irish government. He invited them to take a seat and they all sat down around his desk.

CHAPTER 13

VALERO — MULVANNEY — BYRNE — THOMPSONS

President Valero had many questions about the Brigade's activities. He needed to know the details of the numbers of men involved in ambushes, the weapons used, how men were deployed in action, and how they captured the barracks. He was full of praise for the brigade and did not show any sign of wanting the fighting slowed down. It was quite the opposite. He wanted the fight expanded. There was a rumour that Valero wanted to stop the war and make a compromise peace but he certainly showed no sign of giving in to the British.

Lyons asked if anything could be done about getting more arms and ammunition, especially ammunition. Valero said he would talk to Mick Connor over this and he would make sure that the necessary funds would be available. No expense would be spared to keep the war going. He had collected millions in America and would get more if needed. The Irish in America were a great help with the funding of the whole movement. He was polite and friendly right through the meeting. He became more serious when told of the executions of I.R.A. prisoners and atrocities against the civilian population.

"How are the people holding up? Will they continue to support us, with food, shelter, and information about enemy movements?" he asked.

"I have no doubt they will," replied Liam Lyons. "They voted for a Republic and don't want Home Rule or Dominion Status anymore. We all swore an oath to the republic when we joined the I.R.A. and intend to fight on until we get it. All we need is good, reliable leadership."

"That is my goal, too," said Mr. Valero. "I will not sell out. How long do ye think ye can keep this war going in the first brigade area?"

Liam found it hard to answer this. "It would depend on the pressure the British put on us. They could flood the area with troops, but hopefully we could fight our way through them to another area and join with the I.R.A. in that area and the British would have to follow us. Anyhow, I don't think they have enough troops for this kind of surge."

Valero still pressed for a time estimate. "Maybe he is trying to slow things," Lyons thought. "We can last about six years I believe."

Valero sat upright in his chair. "Great," he replied. "But you are probably exaggerating I would say, but I will take your word for it." With that it was time to end the meeting. He got up from the table and shook hands again with the men and wished them a safe trip down to their area. Mick Connor arrived and after a few words with Valero he left with the men. They went to Rathgar, and spent the night with an aunt of the Sullivans who owned a large house there. It was a safe house that was never suspected.

The next day they went to see Dick Mulvanney, Chief of Staff of the I.R.A. Mick introduced them to each other. They went through the usual pattern of questions about the brigade. Dick was very precise and wanted to know even the smallest details. He praised the men and it was obvious he had a warm regard for Liam Lyons. "I have a new scheme of organization." he said. "That Mick approves of. We want to group the brigades into divisions right around the country."

"Too many areas are far too slack. We have to spread the war so that the British cannot concentrate more troops against the more active areas. A divisional commander and his staff will have control over several brigades across county boundaries and will be able to order men into action and get arms and ammunition for a big ambush for example. There will be a divisional flying column that will take the fight into weaker areas. I know you have worked with your neighbouring brigades, Liam, on a few occasions already, and have the confidence of these men.

So you could develop this plan further. What do you think?"

"I would hate to leave my old brigade but will do so if that is the order. We will have to travel over a much larger area, and communication will be harder. However, I believe we can overcome the difficulties involved. The basic idea is good. One brigade might have more ammunition than a neighbor and the next brigade more grenades and by pooling their resources, become a better fighting force. The intelligence officer would have access to the resources of several brigades. How soon do you plan to do this reorganization?"

"We plan to send an officer from G.H.Q. to set it up in about a month. Until then ye can carry on as before," said Dick.

"I hope we can land the guns promised. We will really need them to operate a division," said Liam.

"That is at an advanced state of planning," said Mick. "We are confident it will succeed. We would like you Liam to take the leadership of the division and John Garry can lead the divisional Flying Column. Think it over for a week and let us know. You can pick your own staff if you like, as you know who the best men for the job are." With that they ended the meeting.

Mick said, "Charlie Byrne would like to see ye." He was the minister for defense. Mick brought them to Byrnes office and introduced them but left right away. He didn't make any small talk with Byrne. Charlie asked plenty questions about the brigade but didn't seem to be as curious as they had met in the other interviews. Charlie had done some splendid fighting in 1916 and had received many wounds. He should have died but lived in spite of the odds. "Will the leadership hold firm until we get the Republic?" Liam asked.

"Well ye can count on me at any rate" he replied. "I will fight until my last bullet is fired and my last shilling is spent." That reassured the men and they said goodbye to Charlie. They met Mick outside the office.

"How was Charlie?" he asked. "Did he ask ye to shoot the British cabinet?" The men were puzzled. They didn't know Byrne went to England in 1918 to shoot the British cabinet, if they tried to force conscription on the Irish people.

"No," said Liam. "But he reassured us he would stand up for the Republic."

"Relations are strained between us," said Mick. "He left the IRB after 1916 but I kept it going and I am the top leader. They call me the 'invisible president' of the Republic. Of course Mr. Valero is the 'visible' president. It shouldn't have caused dissension but you know how it goes sometimes."

"There is none of that tension in our brigade," said Liam. "We are all comrades in arms and ready to die for one another."

"Enough said," replied Mick. "I have one more task for ye to test a new machine gun."

A taxi pulled up at the curb and they drove to a house in Wicklow, owned by a rich sympathizer. It was an ideal place to test the new Thompson submachine gun invented in America and smuggled into Ireland by two American officers. The gun came too late for World War I but a market was needed and Ireland was at war and crying out for weapons. An Irish financier named Fortune-Ryan had helped finance the project and five hundred of the weapons were waiting in a warehouse in the Bronx. They were expensive, about two hundred dollars each, and when payment was made they would be shipped to Ireland. The movement had the money, after all that was collected in America by Valero.

The gun was deadly at fifty yards, firing hundreds of bullets a minute, ideal for ambushes and street fighting in towns. It could be fired from the shoulder. When the taxi reached the house, they all got out. Dick Mulvanney was there and a few members of Connor's squad. The squad was Mick's private force. He used it to wipe out informers and intelligence agents. The house owner invited them out the back of the house to a field where several stacks of bricks were piled up. Dick brought the gun out of the house with the ammunition loaded already.

"Who wants to fire this thing?" he asked. "I hear you country fellows are great shots. Show the Dublin boys how it is done." He got a dirty look from the squad leader, a Dublin man.

John Sullivan stepped forward and took the gun in his hands. "I'll do it," he said. He took careful aim at a pile of bricks fifty yards away, pulled the trigger, and smashed the bricks to bits. Everyone cheered. They all got a chance to fire including the squad leader. They were all agreed that they could use the gun in combat.

"Allright," said Mick. "I will order a batch for Dublin and the first brigade." They stopped for lunch in the sympathizer's house. A friendly conversation started between the squad men and the first brigade men. The squad wanted to hear the accounts of the actions in the first brigade. They explained about their activities, and how dangerous every assignment was. They had to operate under the noses of the British patrolling the streets. During any action a British lorry could come around the corner and wipe them out with machine gun fire. They had to shoot quickly and make a quick getaway. They had wiped out most of the important British secret service men on Bloody Sunday 1920, from which the British never really recovered.

The squad had a headquarters in the city centre from which they operated. They posed as carpenters, but if any customers came, the squad pretended they were too busy and re-directed the customers elsewhere. They invited the country boys to visit them before returning to the country.

CHAPTER 14

HELPING THE SQUAD

The next day Lyons and the Sullivans visited the city centre and dropped in to see the squad. They found twelve men there ready for any eventuality. They were all armed with revolvers and pistols but didn't necessarily carry the weapons on them. They had plenty hiding places for them which they could reach at a moment's notice. The leader McConnell introduced the country men from the first brigade. They all shook hands and a spirited conversation began.

There was a man there from Galway called Meade. He had arrived in Dublin two weeks before on a special assignment to look for Egan and his gang. Egan was an R.I.C. man from the west of Ireland. He hated the I.R.A. and did his best to smash the movement. He was moved to Dublin and given a special gang of R.I.C. undercover men from hot-spots around Ireland. They hoped to seek out, capture and kill I.R.A. members in Dublin, especially men who came in to see Mick Connor, looking for guns and ammunition and bringing him money for Sinn Fein. So far Micks's intelligence service had not identified Egan or any of the gang. It was now a top priority to locate these fellows and eliminate them.

Every day Meade walked the streets with an intelligence officer from Connor's office in Crow street. They had a tip off from a spy inside the British lines, who said Egan was a R.I.C. man but had no further information and of course had no photo of Egan. That was why Meade was brought up from Galway in the hope that he would find Egan.

On the same day that the first brigade men visited the squad headquarters, Meade got a lucky break. He was walking down Dame Street when he saw a tall man of about six feet tall, questioning some civilians who were standing up against the wall. He noticed some other men lurking around, whom he concluded were Egan's men. He recognized the man as Egan who had chased him around Galway. He had cornered Meade once, roughed him up but let him go.

"I'm in two minds about you, Meade," he said. "The next time I meet you might not end too well for you."

Meade crossed the road, hoping Egan didn't notice him. Egan was too busy with his questioning to notice, so Meade hurried to get the squad men across the Liffey and his colleague informed the Crow street office. It was decided right away to attack Egan's group with as many men as they could muster.

Meade burst into the squad's headquarters and shouted, "Hurry, quick, I found Egan and his gang! Come right away with the guns and maybe we can get him once and for all."

McConnell ordered his men into action. He looked at the first brigade men. "Ye are not obliged to participate as ye are not Dublin brigade members, but if ye want to we will give ye guns."

"Count us in," they replied. So the squad gave them each a revolver and ammunition. They all got on bicycles which they would return later. They all cycled across the Liffey to Dame Street. Egan was still there questioning civilians and didn't realize the squad had arrived to get him.

The squad men and Liam Lyons approached on the northern side of the street, but the Sullivans got off their bikes on the southern side. The squad opened fire and Egan dropped down. Two more of his men returned the fire. They were tough and there was no surrender sought by the gang. All three fired back at the squad. Then two gang members fired at the squad from the southern side of the street. They didn't notice the Sullivans sneak up behind them.

James and John shot them dead. Egan and his men were all wounded by now but still firing back.

Just then there was the sound of a British lorry of Auxies hurrying to the scene around College Green. The I.R.A. men were not equipped to fight the Auxies so McConnell blew his whistle as the signal to retreat. They all sped away on their bicycles, up Dame Street, right on Parliament Street, and across the Liffey to the squad's headquarters.

Egan was badly wounded, as were his two nearest colleagues. They were taken to the main hospital where they spent weeks before recovering before being discharged. His two men across the street were taken away to the morgue.

The squad leader congratulated his men on the partial success of the operation and thanked the country lads for their help. "I suggest ye get out of Dublin as soon as possible," he said.

"We will," said Lyons. "Tomorrow." They got a tram back to their lodgings in Rathgar. Mick Connor was already there with the Galway man. Mick was delighted with the outcome. "Egan will not bother us for some time. Maybe he will give up and decide it is not worth it, fighting the squad."

"We must get you out of Dublin as soon as possible," he told the Galway man. "I have a friend a priest who will loan you a clerical outfit. You can dress as a priest and travel with a doctor I know, with a car and a permit to travel."

He thanked the Sullivans and Liam Lyons. "It was above and beyond the call of duty to fight," he said. "Ye are true patriots. John Garry wants ye back right away, so I suggest ye leave tomorrow by train. I will send some squad men to see to it ye get safely on that train at Kingsbridge. I presume ye gave the revolvers back to the squad. It is better to go unarmed and bluff as before."

"We gave the guns back Mick although to tell the truth we really miss them. We would prefer death than to be captured by that brutal Sussex regiment," said Liam.

The next day the Galway man left with the doctor and the first brigade men left by train. Three squad men made sure they got safely on the train. There were some British agents on the platform but they suspected nothing. The doctor and Meade had a puncture in a small town, just outside the R.I.C. barracks. Before they could even start changing the wheel, two R.I.C. men came over and helped. The doctor showed his pass. When they saw the "priest" they became respectful, being all Catholics. They replaced the wheel and the "priest" gave them his "blessing" before leaving. It was hard to keep from laughing, but they laughed heartily when they got outside the town.

"By God," said the doctor. "You are a natural for a career in Holy Orders. That blessing you had it all off."

"Goodness knows I saw it often enough," he replied. They reached their own area in a few hours.

Mick Connor sent a coded message to John Garry to expect Lyons and the Sullivans at a certain railway station. Garry brought the Flying Column into the area. He himself and five other men patrolled the platform, with revolvers in their pockets. The train arrived on time and the men left the train. They headed straight for brigade headquarters, where a hearty breakfast awaited them.

"I hope ye put them in the picture in Dublin," said Garry.

"We did," said Liam. "And we can expect to be very busy in the next few weeks, trying to get guns and ammunition ashore. A big ship is on the way from Italy with twenty thousand rifles and loads of ammunition and machine guns and grenades. They will be landed in our area as we have a brigade with a coast and some harbours."

"Some of our men are fishermen and will go out to the ship, which will anchor off the coast and bring the guns ashore. We will have to use every available, transport to get the stuff moved inland to dumps prepared especially beforehand to receive the stuff. Some of the stuff will go to the surrounding brigades. We will be all one soon when the Division is formed. I will be the divisional commander and you, John, will lead a divisional Flying Column."

"It all sounds great," said Garry. "But there is many a slip between the cup and the lip. I hope we don't have a repeat of the 1916 gun running disaster when the cargo was sunk outside Cork Harbour."

"No," said Liam. "We are better organized now and the people are behind us. We can also expect a delivery of five hundred Thompson sub-machine guns from America, but I don't know where these will be landed. Probably Dublin or the west. We test fired them in Wicklow and we asked Mick to go ahead and get them for us. They will be great for close quarter fighting. They fire hundreds of bullets per minute."

"It sounds great, Liam, "said Garry. "We better keep on the bright side. Security will be a big problem. It will be a miracle if the British don't get word of this. Look at all the men we have to put in the picture beforehand. A pilot will have to travel with the ship and pilot it to the drop-off area. Then we have to arrange small boats and men to offload the stuff and bring it to land. There we will have to arrange motor cars and maybe some lorries to transport the arms inland to dumps. We will need a protective screen of men to guard the area while the unloading is in progress. Then we have to arrange routes to the nearby brigades and loads of dumps to hide everything. There we have to organize different groups of men to keep the British in their barracks. All this in one night. If we succeed we will free Ireland. If we fail I don't know where that leaves us. I always thought smaller consignments would be better."

"I know it is a mighty task," said Liam. "But we have to try. One last push and this could end the war."

"Allright then," said Garry. "Let us start the preparations."

CHAPTER 15

AMBUSH AT KNOCKNACROY

Liam Lyons and John Garry headed for the coastal area where they planned to bring in the arms. They had to inform the local company commander who now became a key man in the whole scheme. They also spoke to the boat owners who would smuggle the stuff ashore. They promised the company commander that he would have the Flying Column behind him and probably a column from the nearby brigades. After about a week in the area checking dumps and for motor cars they could use, they were satisfied they could do no more except wait for the arms ship to come. As soon as the date came from Dublin they would inform the local commander and bring the Flying Column there to ensure a safe landing and distribution of the weapons. They then summoned a brigade council meeting to ensure a continuation of the war.

Garry asked O'Dowd the brigade intelligence chief if he had any new information about British troop movements. He replied that he found out about a convoy of four lorries that traveled between two large towns on the edge of the first brigade area. One town was in the first brigade area and the other in the second brigade area. He said there was a good ambush position inside the second brigade area.

"We will have to get approval from O'Donoghue the second brigade Brigadier if we can use his territory for an attack," said Garry.

"I know him," said Lyons. "And he is a reasonable man. Besides with the coming reorganization into divisions, maybe it would be a good start before it becomes official. I will go to meet him and maybe we can launch a combined attack, using both flying columns."

"That would be great," said John Garry. "Maybe he has more stuff than we have, especially things we are short of." John Dowd said. "These British convoys often include an armoured car and we will need a mine to get this otherwise the Vickers machine gun might prove too much for us."The British had begun to use armoured cars to reinforce their convoys. On a few occasions already, ambushes had to be called off because a complete victory and capture of weapons could not be achieved, because of the armoured cars. The first brigade had a good mine building and mine laying team and now had a few mines ready. The second brigade also had a few mines and between them enough to attack the convoy.

Liam Lyons went to see O'Donoghue a few days later and he gave his support.

"Ye can have our brigade flying column but we could use some more grenades," he said.

"We could use some extra ammunition," said Lyons so they agreed to exchange .303 ammunition for grenades.

A date was set for the ambush. They picked a stretch of road running east-west for about five hundred yards. The terrain was rocky, with some small hills and hollows, some walls that would give cover. There was a small wood to the north of the road and another to the south. The men could hide here until the approach of the British was signaled.

It was the first week of June 1921 and the weather was glorious, sunshine every day and unusual for Ireland, almost no rain. This weather suited the British more than the I.R.A. The days were long and bright and the I.R.A. could not count on the cover of darkness until 10 P.M.. It would be light again around 5 A.M.. The fields became dry and hard, and British vehicles could now use them and all the side roads without getting stuck. They had made several big round-ups trying to trap the flying columns. They would camp out and not return to barracks for a week.

But it was all in vain. Each time the columns outsmarted them; and they went back empty handed. They always arrested people, but usually the wrong people.

The ambush was set for June 5th, 1921. Both columns rose early for breakfast and marched from six miles away roughly and were at the site by 8 A.M.. The grenades and ammunition were exchanged as planned. O'Donoghue deployed his men north of the road in four sections of fifteen men each. Section one was at the western end, with section two fifty yards to the east of this.

Section three was fifty yards farther east, with section four about seventy yards further east and guarding the eastern flank.

John Garry deployed his men in similar fashion with fifteen men in each section. Section one was under Dwyer on the western flank. Next came section two under Lyons, then section three under James Sullivan, and section four under John Sullivan on the eastern side. John Garry and O'Dowd positioned themselves between section two and three. On the north side O'Donoghue and his vice Brigadier were located between section two and three. It was agreed that commandant Lyons would have the final say over a possible retreat if necessary. Then each column would escape in different directions if necessary.

The Lewis gun with O'Brien was attached to Lyons section. There was also a Lewis gun north of the road in section three. Four lorries were expected and a possible armoured car. There was no way to know where the armoured car would be. It could be anywhere. Mines were laid five altogether, in the hope of blowing up the enemy vehicles. The far western mine would be detonated as soon as the first vehicle reached their position. The other mines were placed about fifty yards apart with the fifth mine about two hundred yards east of the first mine. It was hoped that this deployment would be good enough to contain the enemy vehicles in the ambush position and blow as many up as possible. It was important to stop the first lorry. If it escaped, it could launch a flank attack or go to the nearest town for reinforcements. The I.R.A. was always outnumbered by the enemy in every brigade and reinforcements could arrive in half an hour. They would have to attack the other vehicles in the convoy regardless if they were over a mine or not.

The column commanders deployed their men showing each section where to take up positions. Then they allowed them to hide in the woods.

No man would be more than one hundred yards from the road directly in front of them. They were ordered to use their ammunition sparingly. Grenade throwers were attached to each section and told to move close enough to the road to throw grenades into the lorries. There was nothing left now except wait for the convoy. Hour after hour passed by but by 2 P.M. the signal was given of the enemy approach. The men dashed into firing positions and lay flat.

The convoy came on slowly into the ambush position from the east. When the head lorry was over the western mine the engineer pressed the plunger. There was a fierce explosion but it only destroyed the lorry's engine. The road under the lorry was over bog and this absorbed a lot of the blast. The soldier's jumped off the lorry and the fight was on. The fouth lorry also stopped over a mine which was detonated and turned it upside down. Some soldiers were killed and the rest jumped off and fired at the I.R.A. The other lorries and the armoured car stopped but not on mines. So all the I.R.A. sections blazed away at them from both sides of the road. The British soldiers took up firing positions using the walls on the sides of the road for cover. It was hard to see any I.R.A. targets but they kept up a heavy fire. There was a Hotchkiss gun in the second lorry but any gunman that tried to use it was shot by accurate fire from the Lyons group, where the Lewis gun was located. The grenade throwers lobbed grenades at the lorries from north of the road killing and wounding a lot of the enemy.

The armoured car was the best hope of success for the British. The gunner blazed away at John Sullivan's section who took cover behind a stone wall. They had to lay flat as the fire was so intense. It was almost like rain. After a while the gunman swung his gun around to fire at section four north of the road. This gave John

Sullivan a chance to get some of his men into a better firing position to stop some soldiers from the fourth lorry who tried moving east to outflank them.

The gunman of the armoured car noticed them and told the driver, "Move a few yards to the west so I can get nearer to the I.R.A. and get into a better firing position." The driver obeyed, but in doing so he drove over the nearest mine. The engineer pressed his plunger and there was a fierce explosion. The armoured car was blown over onto its side, and the gunner knocked down.

He tried to get up but was shot by John Sullivan's section. This event took the heart out of the British resistance. A lot of these men had no desire to die in Ireland after surviving the trenches in France. They had seen many of their comrades die and more get wounded. An ambush always gave the advantage to the attackers and the ground was chosen especially for this. The shock effect was always great. The first fifteen minutes was often decisive. If the ambush didn't work as planned the I.R.A. would end it and retreat. John Garry used his megaphone to call on the British to surrender. He promised them to spare their lives and they knew he would keep his word as this regiment had not committed any atrocities.

The highest ranking officer was a major from the third lorry. He raised a white flag.

Garry called a ceasefire and the whole I.R.A. group obeyed at seeing the white flag. "Throw down your rifles," he ordered. "And then stand against the lorries with hands raised." They obeyed right away. The I.R.A. men approached the road with caution and seized the weapons. They collected seventy rifles, many revolvers, thousands of rounds of ammunition, boxes of grenades and a Hotchkiss machine gun. The bodies of the dead were pulled to one side and also the wounded, who were attended to by medics from both sides. Then the lorries were burned. Paraffin and petrol had been supplied by the local company. They were also given the job of hiding the guns and all the captured stuff except for the ammunition which was distributed among the flying columns.

O'Donoughue led his column away to the north and Garry his men to the south. Garry and his men reached billets about 6 P.M. where a welcome meal awaited them. After the meal they all rested, guarded by the local company. They caught up on their sleep but planned to get up again at midnight and march under cover of darkness to the wild, mountainous area of the brigade, where they would be safe from British patrols. There was a great pride in the column now and they hoped for victory in the near future.

CHAPTER 16

PEACE AT LAST

The month of June continued with dry warm weather every day. Everyone could enjoy the sunshine and there was no sign of the British at least not in the wild area where the column was billeted. One day a dispatch came from Dublin for Garry and Lyons and O'Dowd to attend a meeting in the second brigade area for the purpose of setting up the division. They spent several days on foot walking to the location for the meeting in a wild area in the second brigade. An officer from Dublin and G.H.Q. came to set up the division and to set up a new staff. There were men there from several brigades covering three counties. There was by no means unanimous agreement about setting up a division, but it had been decided at G.H.Q. and was no longer something that could be stopped. Nobody seemed to want to take a position on the divisional staff as it meant leaving their own brigades at least some of the time, however, after much discussion, Lyons, Garry, O'Dowd, and O'Donoughue agreed to join the staff. Lyons would become divisional commander, with Donoughue as his deputy. Garry would train and lead a divisional flying column and O'Dowd would be the chief intelligence officer. There was a lot of moaning about lack of ammunition and weapons in general and they wanted to know why Mick Connor or Valero never visited their brigades.

"Where was the arms ship that was promised?" asked one brigadier. "By God," he said. "We started this war with hurling sticks but we will have to finish it with fountain pens."

"Why wasn't the fight spread more evenly around Ireland?" another man asked. "Why doesn't Connor remove ineffective officers?" About half of the counties had done little or nothing.

After about two days the meeting ended. The officer from Dublin went back there to make it all official. The men at the meeting went back to their areas until they would get official confirmation of their new appointments.

There were rumours of peace circulating, even mentioned in the newspapers. Lloyd George was making private approaches to Mr. Valero using Archbishop Clune from Australia as a go-between. Smuts of South Africa was also playing a role to get peace. There had been an attempt at peace at the end of 1920 after Bloody Sunday but it fell through as Lloyd George demanded a surrender of arms by the I.R.A. This time he didn't ask for a surrender of arms but some kind of truce would probably be needed before any negotiations started.

The first brigade held a council meeting to discuss the situation. They didn't plan on any action in the immediate future as they wanted to preserve ammunition for the expected arrival of the arms ship. They retrieved the unexploded mines from Knocknacroy but continued to build more mines. O'Dwyer was to take the Brigadier job when Lyons moved to the division and two new flying columns would be formed one under James Sullivan and the other under John. They sent a dispatch to Dublin to enquire about the arms ship. A few days later Mick Connor sent a dispatch to say the whole project was called off. It had been compromised somehow. British intelligence found out about it. The machine guns would not come either as they were grabbed by the F.B.I. in the warehouse in New York before they could be shipped to Ireland.

John Garry was furious. "I told ye this would happen," he said. "It would have been better to smuggle on a smaller scale like Childers did in 1914 at Howth and made possible the rebellion of 1916. There could be a British spy at headquarters for all we know. All our planning work was in vain."

"We have to carry on as before," replied Liam Lyons. "We are well armed right now. I'm sure some small scale smuggling of guns can be arranged especially from Wexford/Waterford area which is nearer to the continent. Anyhow by just staying in existence we are a thorn in the side of the British. They have to beat us. When the days are shorter we can start ambushing them again."

"I suppose you are right," replied John. "It was just our hopes were raised so high with the prospect of the arms ship arriving. What we could have done with those weapons!Maybe that Brigadier at the divisional meeting was right after all. We could finish this war with fountain pens."

July was even hotter, and drier than June. Farmers had no problem saving hay that year. About the 4th of July a dispatch came from Dublin. Brigadier Lyons opened it and read the message. "A truce will take effect on July 11th." There was no other explanation. They just had to stop the fighting.

Lyons read the message over again to make sure he was not mistaken. Then he handed it to John Garry. "You are right, Liam," he said. "We have to stop on the 11th."

"What could it mean?" he asked. "There was no warning that this would happen. I wonder how long will it last? I can only assume that it is a temporary measure. We have not won the war yet. I don't think we are even halfway there. Think of all the plans for the arms ship and the machine guns. So behind the scenes peace was being negotiated, and we killing ourselves with our smuggling plans." No Brigadier got any notice about a truce they learned later.

"I don't like one bit of it," said Liam Lyons. "What will we tell the rank and file?

Will we dismiss them all? What will they do? For a lot of them the column has become their life. What can they do now? Jobs are scarce around here. If they emigrate we will lose them for good."

"The whole approach could be a trick," said John Garry, "with the intention of dividing us. They will not give us a 32-county independent republic but probably offer some compromise deal. This will tempt some of the I.R.A. to accept and some of the people. A dangerous situation will be created that could lead to civil war."

"I hope you are wrong, John" said Liam. "I suggest we inform the men and give them two weeks off starting July 11th but bring them back for training again to keep them all sharp. Maybe we can do a little smuggling of weapons, although the truce will forbid that. I'm sure the British intelligence service, will be busy during the truce trying to identify active I.R.A. members to make it easier to arrest them when the fighting resumes. I will warn the men to keep as low as profile as possible."

They assembled the column on the morning of July 11th. John Garry explained the situation to them and how they would have two weeks off before resuming military duty. The men looked surprised but accepted the instructions of their commander. Every battalion in the brigade was represented in the column so they bade each other farewell and went back to their own parishes. The Sullivans reached home about 6 P.M. that evening. Their mother thought she was looking at ghosts. They were thin, unshaven, with longish hair and in need of a change of clothes. Their parents embraced them. They were so glad they came back alive, unlike other families that were not so lucky.

"We are so glad of what ye did for Ireland," said their father. "ye kept up the tradition handed down by your Fenian grand-father."

"Ye must be ravenous," said their mother, and she prepared a hearty meal for them. They sat at the kitchen table and ate their fill.

Some neighbours heard of their return and came in to con-gratulate them and welcome them home.

"How long will ye stay?" their mother asked.

"We will stay two weeks" said James. "But we have to go back to the column then to keep training."

"I thought the war is over and that ye have won," their father said.

"No," replied John. "It is just a truce. It could end any day. We have to fight on to get the Republic if necessary." Their mother looked sad, but that was in the future.

For now they could enjoy the break. The Sullivans didn't know it, but it was the end of the War of Independence.

The Sullivans enjoyed a wonderful two weeks. They visited neighbours, friends, cousins and the local publican, where the early meetings of the company were held. The publican put two pints of Guinness in front of them.

"Ye are men now, he said, "and entitled to some of life's pleasures." They got a lift in a car the local company had acquired from a British judge. A group of Auxies tried to stop them on the street. "That belongs to our side, the Auxie said.

"Would ye like to take it back?" James replied keeping his right hand firmly on the revolver in his pocket.

Another auxie said to his mate, "Forget it. There is a truce. We can get it when the war starts again."

"That might not be so easy" John said as they drove past the Auxies. "I wonder if they were in the group we ambushed," said James.

"If the fight starts again they will certainly recognize us," said John.

"They will not take us alive," said James.

After two weeks they returned to the column for training. The talks with the British government started in July when Mr. Valero went to London with a few other leaders.

The terms offered were so disgusting he rejected them out of hand, however they didn't go back to war as the British kept in touch with Valero and new talks began in October. Valero didn't go this time to London, but sent over Mick Connor and four other men to negotiate. They were told not to sign anything with partition or an oath of allegiance.

However Lloyd George played his trump card on the 5th December. He threatened an "immediate and terrible war" if they didn't accept the terms on offer. The delegation caved in. They believed the threats. Who wants an immediate and terrible war? They brought the treaty back to Dublin. The cabinet split, the Dail split, and a majority of the people later voted for the treaty. It was exactly like John Garry had predicted. It was all a British trick. They could not win the war but they could win the peace. Sadly Ireland drifted slowly into Civil War.

CPSIA information can be obtained
at www.ICGtesting.com
Printed in the USA
LVHW03s0253060918
589326LV00016B/676/P